ONE

RANDALL HUDSON SCANNED the faces gathered around the Table of Knowledge at Debbie's Restaurant. The small diner hosted a variety of characters every day from early morning to mid-afternoon. The food was good, the company friendly, and the prices reasonable.

He held up his coffee cup for the passing waitress. She filled it with the steaming hot liquid, then those of all the others at the table. Service here was always good, and they never ran out of his favorite blend. Black. He didn't care what kind. A good cup of ink was all he needed to kick-start his day.

"You got more guests coming out to the ranch today?" Earl asked the same question every week.

"Yep. Matthew is there greeting them right about now." He looked at his watch. It was old school, wind-up, and didn't even have a battery. His daddy had given it to him before he died, but it still ran like it did when it was made sixty years ago. Strong and consistent.

"You're not there to greet 'em?" Ned, one of the old cowboys, tilted his head.

"Nope. Matthew is the Operations Manager for the ranch now. I'll see them tomorrow when I run the trail ride." He took another sip, enjoying the feel of the steamy liquid as it slid down his throat.

"He's growed up quite nicely. Needs himself a young woman. I've got a granddaughter just about the right age." Earl was a longtime friend, but his granddaughter lived in California.

"You need one, too, Randall." Harris's grizzled lips smirked as he sipped his coffee. That's all anyone ever called him. Nobody even knew his first name. "Maybe some cute young filly will trot off that bus and straight into your heart." They all laughed together, and Randall just shook his head.

"Matthew and I are just fine. Kate was the love of my life. When she died, I buried my love with her. I have no desire to fall in love again." Randall wrinkled his brown eyes, lines growing from the corners of those eyes to his temples. Years spent in the sun had created them, but each one was well-earned.

"Awe. Ain't that sweet." They snickered around him, but he knew it was friendly. They had all known Kate and mourned with him when she died.

He scratched his jaw as they cajoled. Randall was born and raised in Texas and had seen all of it. From the panhandle to the Rio Grande. Through four hundred miles of desert, the oil basin, along the Gulf Coast, and everywhere in between. He had sat at the table of powerful CEO's, high up in the skyscrapers of Dallas and Houston. And he shared coffee with down-to-earth good ol' boys who could write a check for a million dollars and not even blink.

The Table of Knowledge was full of these good ol' boys. As down to earth as if they didn't have a dime to their names. Randall was one of them.

NORA HILLS, TEXAS | PREQUEL

A MATTER OF

RENA BELL YEAGER

A Matter of Trust

© 2025 by Rena Bell Yeager

All Scripture is quoted from the New International Version.

THE HOLY BIBLE, NEW INTERNATIONAL VERSION®, NIV® Copyright © 1973, 1978, 1984, 2011 by Biblica, Inc.® Used by permission. All rights reserved worldwide.

Note: This novel is a work of fiction. Names, characters, places, and incidents are either products of the author's imagination or used fictitiously. All characters are fictional, and any similarity to people living or dead, is purely coincidental.

Edited by: Kim Richardson, Tri-Epsilon Productions, LLC

Cover by: Emilie Haney, EAHcreative.com

ISBN – ebook - 979-8-9985066-0-4

ISBN – print - 979-8-9985066-1-1

PIXLEY KNOB PRESS

Generations of Hudsons had built the ranch up to what it today. Twenty-five thousand acres of the best real estate in the area. When his wife suggested adding a resort for people who wanted to see and experience a working ranch, he balked. He didn't want strangers wandering all over his land, getting into trouble. But when she and their son, Matthew, built a solid business plan, he relented. Now she was gone, and Matthew ran the resort.

"Randall, you've been alone too long." Ned's comment broke his thoughts.

"Ned, the last thing I need is a cute young filly. Or maybe you're hoping there will be one for you."

They all guffawed, Ned's face turning red.

Randall stood and drained the last few drops of coffee down his throat, then set the cup down with a salute. "Guys, I'll see you Monday morning." He knocked twice on the round table and settled his well-worn Stetson on his head.

"See ya." They all knocked on the table, and Randall walked out the door.

The late March sun was hot today, but then this was Texas. Randall strolled to his truck, his boots thumping on the wooden porch before hitting the gravel parking lot. Thirty-five hundred ccs of diesel power were wrapped in dust so thick you almost couldn't tell it was black. Time for a car wash. He would have one of the guys at the ranch spray it off.

He slipped onto the leather seat, set his hat on the passenger side, and put his key in the ignition. It had a lot of miles on it for a truck that was only five years old, but it held his heart. Kate bought the truck for him as a birthday gift before she got sick. They had taken their last trip to the hospital in this truck, and he could still smell her memory. Her essence. Her spirit. Her drive and determination. Her bright laugh and kind smile. Her sunshine-yellow hair and sweet shampoo.

Every trip to town kept her with him, memories of their love, his companion.

He patted the steering wheel a few times in salute before turning the key, bringing the truck to life. Yeah, he was lonely, but he didn't need a new woman. Earl and the guys were way off base.

* * *

RACHEL STARED at her computer screen. ACCESS DENIED. Her company laptop had just rebooted and locked itself while she was sending an email to one of her teams, leaving behind a blank white screen containing that one glaring message front and center. This had to be a glitch of some kind, or maybe a malware attack. There had been a pop-up on their internal messaging app, but she hadn't had time to read it before her laptop locked up. Thank God she wasn't in the middle of an internet meeting with a client. But she had lost her email, and would have to recreate the message. She hoped she could remember her thoughts.

Following normal IT protocol, she rebooted everything to try again. The Windows screen appeared as if trying to load, then disappeared and displayed the same blank screen with the same message. ACCESS DENIED.

"What is going on? Have we been hacked?" Talking to herself, she tilted her head and rebooted the computer again. She had heard of several companies in the past year that had been victims of sophisticated cyber-attacks. Was Dencor now on their hit list?

She pushed her hair off her face, the curly lock of blue falling over her forehead again. She worked from her home office, only going into the company office in New York City a couple of times a month to meet with upper management.

Picking up her company cell phone, she dialed the number to their help desk.

"We're sorry. Service is currently unavailable at this time."

She called one of her team members and received the same message.

Shaking her head, she considered her next steps, when her personal cell phone rang with the theme song from *Happy Days*. Frustrated at the interruption, she tapped the phone to answer on speaker.

"Mom! Turn on the local news channel." Annie's voice was urgent.

"What? Why? I have a bit of a crisis here."

"Yes. You do. Turn on the news now. Dencor was just raided by the FBI."

Rachel picked up the remote and pointed it toward her television. The screen filled with images of FBI agents raiding her corporate office building in downtown Manhattan. The caption at the bottom caused her to freeze. FRAUD.

She watched the news report for several minutes, but the story stayed in a loop with the same few images over and over. Still not knowing any more than she did a half hour ago, she flipped to another channel to see the same story. A third channel also had the story splayed across the screen, all with the same images. Federal agents going in and out of the building, which was surrounded by black SUVs, vans, and a myriad of blinking lights.

Rachel stared at the TV for several minutes, not knowing what to do. What had happened at Dencor? Her employer held contracts with large organizations across the United States. Rachel led highly talented project teams who worked with the companies to integrate systems containing sensitive data.

Rachel hadn't seen a hint of impropriety. But the opportunity was definitely there.

The TV reporter zoomed in on two men being escorted out of the building in handcuffs. It was the CEO and CFO of Dencor. Fortunately, there were three layers between her position and the C-suite. She hoped she wouldn't be pulled into that drama. She used her personal cell phone to call her help desk, looking for more information than what the news reports were stating. The call was immediately forwarded to a message, which stated that all network access was currently frozen. More information would be available at a later date. Rachel sighed and called her vice president. There was no answer there, either.

She called Annie back and gave her an update. There wasn't much to tell. She was locked out of everything. But she was glad that she hadn't been at the office when it was raided. If federal authorities were scouring the building, they likely had the remaining leadership sequestered. It would be a long day for them.

Unable to do anything else for the moment, she switched to a movie channel, hoping to find some relief from the worries swirling through her mind. But it was a sappy romance. Mindless, cookie-cutter drivel that didn't hold her attention. So she surfed to a cooking show. At least this channel could occupy her mind with a new way to cook chicken. Nah, she didn't need that, either. She flipped through the channels again and again.

Her laptop stared at her from her coffee table, taunting her with its blank screen. Her company cell phone sat next to it, silently begging for attention. Rachel hoped it was a temporary thing, but the burning pain in her gut told her that life had just changed for over a thousand employees of Dencor. And she was one of them. Was she out of a job?

•—————————•

"YOU KNOW WHAT YOU NEED, Mom? You need a vacation."

It had been two weeks since the raid, and Rachel had already cleaned the house, taken her car into the shop for an oil change, and reorganized her closet. She had taken three large boxes of clothes and items she didn't use anymore to a local charity. Now she sat at her dining table, tapping her fingernails in boredom.

"What I need is a job." She stared out her living room window. A freighter tooted as it pushed its way upstream. The Hudson River was only two blocks away from her four-bedroom home. "I can't believe Dencor was closed by the FBI. I've been with them for fifteen years. I never saw any hint of fraud at any level. It must have been cleverly hidden."

"What you need, Mother, is to get away. How long has it been since you took a vacation? Oh, right. You haven't had one. You went straight to work after Dad left, and you haven't stopped."

"You mean, since I kicked your cheating father out." She cringed at her own statement. "Sorry, Annie, but you know it's the truth."

"Yes, I know. And I don't blame you for doing that. You took care of me, making sure I finished high school with honors and got good college scholarships that took me all the way through my master's degree at NYU."

"That was my job, Annie. As your mother."

"And I am a grown woman now. Your job is done. Let's go somewhere and relax for a few days. Just a few."

Rachel studied Annie's pleading eyes. The market was already flooded with displaced employees. It would be hard to find another position anywhere. And despite labor laws, Rachel knew that hiring managers would take one look at her and pass. They wanted young and pliable. Not experienced.

Rachel's daughter sat on the sofa, brushing her blonde bangs out of her eyes, which were the same color as Rachel's, pool-water blue. In fact, Rachel and Annie's baby pictures looked almost identical, except for the time frame. They had a close bond, and had stood up for each other over the years.

"I have some time coming, Mom. Let's take a vacation together. I'll help with the expense. You have given everything in you to either me or your job for the last fifteen years. It's time to do something nice for yourself. Maybe you'll meet some hot young guy."

Rachel wasn't up to a trip, and she wouldn't let Annie pay for it, but she would humor her daughter and let her creative marketing brain come up with ideas. It would have to be something different. Vegas was definitely out. Not a cruise or a beach vacation. No mountain cabins. No brawny lifeguards or lumberjacks to swoon over. And no hot young guy.

TWO

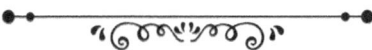

RANDALL STRODE out to the stable where his guests were waiting for today's trail ride. Most of them were in their twenties or thirties and were obviously tourists in their trendy jeans and athletic shoes. Some even wore shorts, since it was warm for March, and he figured there would be a few complaining of sore legs later tonight. He shook his head. The ranch website provided detailed information on attire they would need for riding. But some guests either ignored the instructions or were young and, in their minds, invincible. Fortunately, the ranch was prepared for such injuries and had a well-stocked mini-clinic.

Randall was strangely excited about meeting his guests today. He had always had a secondary role on the resort, allowing Matthew to run the operation. So he was not present when the resort bus arrived from the airport the day before. But he felt a buzz in his soul today. One that he couldn't explain. Something new was going to happen, and he found he was ready.

He gave preliminary instructions to all the riders, then

nodded to the cowhands standing nearby who would assist the riders as they mounted up. Most of the visitors were nimble enough to swing their legs over without assistance, but some were too short or had physical limitations. They had mounting blocks the riders could stand on that would allow everyone to easily reach the first stirrup, striving to make all the activities as accessible as possible.

Working his way down the line of the dozen or so riders, he made a final check of the cinches and stirrups himself, since he was leading the ride. Halfway down the line, he looked up into the most beautiful eyes he had ever seen and was taken aback for a moment. The woman's curves and God-given gray high-lights gave him a hint at her age, but it was the blue streak in her hair reflected again in the blue of her eyes that made him stop. He was reminded of the last trip he had taken with his wife before she died. The blue was the color of the Caribbean waters, and flowed just as gently as her hair waved in the wind.

There was not a stitch of makeup on her face, yet beauty shone from the anticipation he saw there. She had a few wrin-kles, but she wore them with confidence and grace. It made him blink.

"You'll want to wear that to protect your beautiful head from the hot sun." He nodded to the straw cowboy hat she held in her hand, and wondered if she had bought it in their gift shop. "I'm Randall. Welcome to the Double H Ranch. Where are you from?"

Rachel shifted in the saddle, smiling as she spoke. "I'm Rachel, and this is my daughter, Annie." She pointed at the rider behind her. "We're from New York, just north of the city. We decided we needed some of your warm sunshine and a change of pace for a few days." Randall adjusted her stirrup, moving her foot slightly to indicate the proper position.

Her jeans and boots were right for the ride, but they had

never been worn. Yet she sat in the saddle as if she was comfortable. He wondered at her background. "You look like you might know what you're doing. You ride?"

"English. I know—it's a lot different from Western, but not so different that I can't sit in the saddle." Rachel grinned back at him. So she wasn't a complete greenhorn. Excellent. Her appeal kicked up a notch.

Randall patted her lace-up riding boot, also noticing that she didn't wear a ring. "Western is different, but I'm sure you will be fine. It's just a slow trail ride over parts of the ranch. I'm glad you came to visit, and I hope you enjoy your stay."

He smiled at her again before moving on to the rider she introduced as Annie, who looked like a younger version of Rachel, sans the blue and gray hair. They had no men with them, and he wondered at their story. The two women passed a strange gaze at each other, the daughter mischievous and the mother wide-eyed.

••———————•••

"BEFORE WE GO ANY FARTHER, I have a few instructions." Randall stopped at a large metal gate and turned in order to be heard.

"It is critical that you stay with this group. This is a working ranch, and if you were to wander off, you could easily get lost or injured. This ranch covers over twenty-five thousand acres. Thirty-nine square miles. It is seven miles long by just over five and a half miles wide. That would be a lot of ground for us to cover if you were to fall off your horse out there or get lost." Randall waived his arm toward the open range.

"We run Angus beef cattle, but we also raise and train horses, as well as normal farm animals, which we use in our dining room for your meals. And of course, we raise fruits and vegetables for the same purpose. We try to be as self-sustaining as possible. Your meal tonight will be a true farm-to-table experience."

He saw Rachel raise her eyebrows at his last statement. She was a city girl. He wondered if she really understood the effort that goes into making the ranch sustainable. Then again, ranchers have been living this way for three hundred years. It was like breathing to him.

"YOU MAY HAVE ALSO SEEN several vineyards on your drive in from the airport. While we don't grow our own grapes, we do serve a selection of local wines at dinner. You may also feel free to sample some at our Sunday afternoon wine tasting."

Randall watched as Rachel and Annie grinned at each other. City women.

He turned and explained further to the group, "You will only see a small portion of the ranch during your stay here. Visitor areas are clearly marked, as are areas that you should steer clear of. Pun intended." There were a few nervous chuckles. "We will appreciate everyone's cooperation."

Randall looked around at the group to observe that they had listened and understood. He stopped when his eyes met Rachel's, his smile growing just a little bit wider. He nodded his head at her and turned to continue on with the tour.

Rachel was obviously an experienced rider. Randall admired her as she sat tall in her saddle, moving in perfect balance with the smooth gait of the Tennessee Walker she rode. He would like to see her in action on an Arabian or Thoroughbred. Or riding hunt/jump at the National Horse Show in Kentucky. Too bad they hadn't met "back in the day," as the saying went. But then again, if that had happened, he might not have met Kate. And he wouldn't have Matthew.

•————•

RACHEL LET her gaze travel over the man leading the trail ride. He had simply introduced himself as Randall, so she didn't know what his role was here at the ranch. But he carried himself with the confidence of a man that had a lifetime of experience. His eyes had looked on her as if he was seeing something new for the first time. And there was a warm message behind his orbs of milk chocolate. Like he had been given a present and was looking forward to opening it.

The ranch was exceptional, far beyond what she had imagined. Rachel admitted to herself that Annie might have had a good idea. While the climate and terrain were different than anything in New York, it was surprisingly peaceful, even in the scorching sun of the afternoon. Randall was right. She did need the hat.

He turned to look at the group, making sure everyone was still with him, and caught her eyes. His gaze made a shiver go up her spine. She couldn't tell how tall he was, since he was riding, but he definitely had strong shoulders. The blue chambray shirt fit snuggly across his back, and he sat in the saddle as if he was born there. Some people had that talent, she knew. It was a sense of balance that held him there, and she envied him just a bit. What would it be like to ride in that saddle with him, with his arms wrapped around her? She smiled inwardly, and maybe a little outwardly. It was a naughty thought, and she had been without companionship for far too long. But she reminded herself she was not here to find a *hot young guy*.

Randall strode directly to her as they dismounted at the

end of the ride. "Did you enjoy the day?" He took her reins, holding the horse but not moving to take him to the barn.

"It was a lovely ride. You have a great stable of horses here."

"I didn't introduce myself properly earlier." He held out his hand to take hers. "I'm Randall Hudson. I own the ranch."

She let him take her hand. "Rachel Wilson. You're the owner?"

"Yes, with my son, Matthew. You may have met him yesterday. But he runs the resort. I'm just the hired help."

Somehow, she didn't think that was quite true. His grin reminded her of a Clint Eastwood smirk. She wondered what lurked behind that handsome smile.

"You have an impressive spread."

"Thank you." He stuttered a moment, looking down for a second before locking on her eyes again. "I was impressed with the way you rode today. Would you like to accompany me to dinner in the dining hall tonight? I usually sit with a few guests a couple of times during the week. I would love the opportunity to get to know you."

Rachel held her breath for a short moment. He was a very handsome man, with his strong jawline and eyes the color of chestnuts at Christmas. She hadn't been to dinner with a man who wasn't a business partner or a client in several years, which was pretty pathetic as she considered his request. Why not? She was here to break out of her routine and have a good time. She tilted her head, letting her hair fall in her eyes before answering. Turning her head toward her daughter, she saw Annie talking to a tall cowboy.

"Annie is welcome to join us. There will be two other couples as well."

"Well, then. We would love to. Thank you for inviting us."

"Great. I will meet you right outside the dining room at six."

Rachel's heart thumped. Was this a date?

• •————————• •

RANDALL'S SON, Matthew, whistled at his father as he came down the stairs of the homestead into the open living space. Randall was dressed in black Wranglers, a white chambray shirt with pearl snaps, and a pearl, silver, and leather bolo tucked under his collar. His black custom-made boots had the perfect shine. He had spent a full hour to make them look like new. He carried his black Stetson in one hand.

"Got a hot date tonight?" Randall chuckled at Matthew's tease. His son was a mirror image of his father at thirty-two. They ran the ranch and other Hudson Holdings businesses together. Randall had not had a date since sickness had taken Kate from them. It had left the family dry and empty.

"I invited a few of our guests to join me tonight. Get to know some of them. You know I do that with each new group." Randall ducked his head to pass by Matthew.

"One of those guests wouldn't happen to be a woman with a blue streak in her hair, would it?" Matthew grinned again, this time wider. Randall knew there would be an inquisition later, but he felt like he was up to the challenge.

"I'm going to be late, Son." Randall straightened his bolo. "See ya later." He winked, and Matthew laughed. His heart beat in his chest to a happy tune, the buzz he felt earlier now louder and stronger.

• •————————• •

RACHEL WONDERED why she had agreed to have dinner with Randall Hudson. She stared at her reflection in the mirror and wondered what he saw. Was it a woman past her prime? A woman with too much flesh in the wrong places? A woman so desperate for company that she would travel fifteen hundred miles in hopes somebody would see some value in her? One thing was for certain. She was not here for a fling. And if Randall Hudson thought she would fall into his arms at the first invitation, he could think again. Even with her naughty thoughts.

Still, she was looking forward to tonight's dinner. He was a handsome man. His salt-and-pepper hair gave him a distinguished look that made her jealous of how easily he wore it. He was physically fit and wore his Wranglers well. And he was obviously successful, with such a large ranch. But Rachel had not been in a relationship since she had thrown her cheating husband out on his ear, and she wasn't sure she was ready to start one now.

Still, it would have been rude to turn down his invitation to dine together. She fastened the pair of dangling blue topaz earrings, which brought out the blue in her eyes and the streak in her hair, then ran her hands down her straight black dress and took a deep breath to soothe her nerves.

"Wow, Mom. You look great."

"Thanks, Annie. I'm a little nervous, and I don't know why." She brushed the blue streak off her forehead. She should have put a clip in it.

"It's just a dinner, Mom. I'll be right there with you. And your hair is beautiful."

They entered the lobby of the visitors' lodge and marveled at the décor. The guests had a choice of staying here, where there were several large guest rooms and a couple of suites, or in one of several cabins located behind the lodge near a creek.

The cabins were more private but also more primitive, even though they each had running water and electricity, and a small kitchen. She and Annie were staying in a cabin.

Rachel made her way alongside Annie to the guest house, entering through double doors. Looking around the lobby, she wondered why they called it a lodge. It would be a great venue for any New York party. Rachel was impressed with the high ceilings, polished tile floors, and tall windows looking out to the wrap-around porch that was filled with wicker chairs, love seats, and rockers. The dining room was to the left of the lobby, and it was equally decorated. It also had three sets of French doors, which had been opened to give a sense of dining outdoors, while retaining the comfort of being indoors. With the March weather in the upper-seventies, it was the perfect setting.

A shadow moved next to Rachel, and she felt Randall's presence before she saw him.

"Good evening, Mrs. Wilson. Annie." He nodded at both of them. "I hope you have enjoyed your first full day here at the Double H." The question in his eyes was hopeful.

"Yes, I have. We have. Very much." She looked up. He stood a full head taller than her five-foot, six-inch self, but it was a good view of his strong jaw and chin, which were clean-shaven. "I haven't ridden in a while, but I'm not as sore as I thought I would be from a two-hour ride. And please, call me Rachel. I haven't been Mrs. Anything in a very long time."

"All right, Rachel. Call me Randall. You look lovely tonight, by the way." His gaze swept over her. "May I escort you to our table?" He held out his elbow for her, completely ignoring her last remark. But his eyes held a new look.

Rachel shivered at his perusal. She hadn't been treated with that kind of deference in years. Maybe never. He placed his hand on the small of her back, and she allowed him to guide her to their table, admiring his profile as they walked. Strong jawline and chin. Bump in his nose. She wondered if it had been broken at some point. She wanted to run her fingers over that bump and the luscious lips below it. And shook her head at the ridiculous thought.

Annie gave her mother a knowing smile before stepping behind them to follow. Rachel raised her eyebrows at her daughter, reminding her that she was not here to find a man.

It proved to be a very comfortable dinner, and not at all awkward like she thought it might be. There were two other couples sitting at their table, and they each told stories about themselves and their thoughts on the ride they had been on earlier.

The meal consisted of steak, which was cooked perfectly to order, baked potato, steamed vegetables, and salad. It was a simple meal elegantly served by wait staff dressed in short waistcoats, black slacks, and shiny black shoes. A drink was never more than half empty, and the waiters made a show of filling them from a foot above the glass, never spilling a drop.

"Tonight's dessert is New York cheesecake with a selection of toppings to choose from. It may not be as New Yorky as your cheesecake back home, but I guarantee it is delicious." Randall grinned as he nodded at the waiter who was bringing around the dessert cart.

"New Yorky? Is that a technical term?" She touched his arm, then pulled it away in embarrassment.

Randall reached for Rachel's hand and covered it with his. "You try the cheesecake and let me know." The other couples at the table smiled as they watched the interaction.

She pulled her hand away and moved it to her lap. Was he flirting with her? She hadn't dated a man since her divorce, having thrown herself into caring for Annie and her work. This was new territory, and she wasn't quite sure how to react. After all, she was fifty-two years old. She wasn't sure what the rules were anymore.

He looked around at the group. "Tomorrow night we will serve a chuck wagon dinner around the campfire. We will be serving stew cooked over the fire in cast-iron pots that have been in the Hudson family for over a hundred years. We will also serve biscuits cooked in Dutch ovens, and of course everyone will be welcome to enjoy our version of the graham cracker, marshmallow, and chocolate dessert."

He turned back to Rachel. "I have business to attend to during the day tomorrow, but I will try to join you at dinner if that is okay." His brown eyes held a hint of hope in them.

Rachel ducked her head and nodded. This was proving to be an eventful trip.

THREE

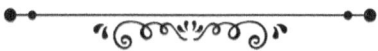

"I TOLD YOU, you would meet a really hot guy!" Annie squealed as they entered their cabin.

"You said a 'hot young guy.' And while Randall is nice looking, he is not young. He is probably close to my age." Rachel thought back to the evening and her first impressions of him.

"First names already. You move fast, Mom." Annie teased her mother.

"This is not New York, Annie. People are much more relaxed down here. And it was just dinner. I bet he does that with each new group of guests. He'll be dining with others at some point, I am sure." Although he did say he would try to meet her at the campfire tomorrow.

Still, Rachel couldn't keep the excitement out of her voice, and Annie picked up on that. "I knew this would be a good trip for you. I can't wait for your update tomorrow!"

"You'll be at the campfire, too."

"Yes, but I think I'm going to be busy." Annie's eyes twinkled.

Rachel wondered about Randall's wife. He wasn't wearing

a wedding ring. Was he divorced? Widowed? Had she been an elegant debutante and Randall the young buck who stole her away? Was she graceful and willowy, her body lithe as she floated over the floor? Rachel looked down at her own body.

What had made Randall ask her to dinner tonight? Was he just being kind? His hand on her back had been warm. His aftershave was more sunshine and less spice. And he was attentive to all of them, but especially to her.

"Mom? Are you there?" Annie waved her hand over Rachel's face. "You look like you are lost in thought. Maybe you'll be dreaming about chestnut-colored eyes tonight." Annie's eyebrows wiggled up and down.

"Good night, Annie."

"Sweet dreams, Mom."

Rachel went into her bedroom and threw herself backwards onto her bed, her heart beating out of her chest. Randall's handsome face filled her mind. Sweet dreams, indeed.

⋅—————⋅

RANDALL TRUDGED INTO THE HOMESTEAD, exhausted after meeting all day with Hudson Holdings board members at their office in San Antonio. He used to enjoy these quarterly meetings where he would receive updates on each of his subsidiaries and discuss goals for the next quarter, as well as the year. But it was starting to become less of a challenge and more of a job. The mental stress bled over into physical stress, and he knew he wasn't a spring chicken anymore. At least that was what he had overheard one of his directors say when they didn't know he was listening. But some of his board members were in their late sixties and still going strong. Maybe it was just the desire that was waning. Or maybe it was a woman with a blue streak in her hair that had him thinking there might be more to life.

Randall stripped out of his business suit, tossing his jacket, starched shirt, and tie onto the bed. He walked into the ensuite bathroom, where he held his hands under the faucet, filled them with water, and splashed his face. Then did it again. And one more time.

A little more refreshed, he searched his closet for his favorite jeans and another chambray shirt. He had several, and they were all showing the passage of time. The worn blue threads were fading at his elbows and around the collar, but it was still the most comfortable shirt he owned. When neatly pressed with just a little bit of sizing, it was still suitable for a night around a campfire with a pretty lady.

He slipped into his chocolate-colored boots and matching belt with a silver and gold buckle, and picked up his favorite brown Stetson, hoping that Rachel would still be out at the campfire.

She had just handed her empty stew bowl to the cowboy who was serving them, still holding a bite of biscuit in her hand. Randall slipped in beside her and watched her face change as she enjoyed that final bite, eyes closed and moaning. He touched the back of her waist lightly to announce his presence, and she jumped, swallowing quickly to keep from choking.

"Enjoying your meal?" He grinned as she tried to recover.

She swallowed hard before speaking. "Heavenly. That's all I've got to say. Pure Heaven."

"We keep a few hogs that we use for our pork sausage and bacon, and we render our own lard, which we use in the biscuits. You can't get any fresher, or taste any better."

"It was amazing to watch the process, or what we saw of it. I didn't know biscuits could be cooked over an open fire, so that was an experience, watching the cook as he placed coals on top and around the Dutch oven." She licked the crumbs from her fingers. "It was so good. Light, flaky, and had just the right amount of golden crust on the top and bottom. My kudos to the chef."

Randall laughed. "Well, he's not a five-star chef from New York, but I bet those guys couldn't do what Cookie does."

"Is his name really Cookie?"

"Nah, that's just a nickname. I think all ranch cooks are called Cookie. His real name is Doug." He hesitated before speaking again. "Do you want to take a walk with me? I can show you the lake at night."

Randall held out his hand, which Rachel took, as they made their way from the campfire to the lake. He loved the feel of her fingers entwined with his. His heart skipped a beat as he thought about starting over in life, spending time with a beautiful woman, and possibly falling in love.

Although it was much too soon to be thinking like that, he did admit to himself that he was looking forward to spending time with her during the few days left of her vacation. The guys at the Table of Knowledge would all want details. They were worse than women.

The moon shimmered over the water, the man in the moon smiling as he looked down on them. The mountains and valleys on the face were easily seen tonight, outlining the eyes, nose, and the knowing expression. He might have even been winking at them.

They stopped at the water's edge. Rachel sighed as the peaceful quiet surrounded them, noise from the campfire at a distance, the crickets and katydids chirping softly. Her eyes glimmered when she blinked and closed them, lifting her face toward Heaven. Randall didn't think he had ever seen anything more beautiful.

"What are you thinking?" His voice was low and made her quake.

"Hm?" Rachel turned to him. "I'm thinking that New York is far away tonight, and I have never found such peace as you have here."

"So don't go home. Stay here another week." It was a sudden thought and maybe he shouldn't have said it out loud, but he wasn't going to take it back.

He watched her sigh. She was facing the sky again, eyes closed, but she wrapped her arms around herself. He wanted to be the one to do that. "I lost my job a couple of weeks ago. That was why I came here. I needed to recoup from the shock. And I hadn't taken a vacation in years. But my budget is slim, and I need to get back to start job hunting again." Her shoulders slumped as she spoke. This was his chance to back out of the invitation.

"I'm sorry to hear that, Rachel." He paused before continuing. "Stay as my guest. I'll check with the hostess, but I think we have a spare cabin open next week. You can have it." He watched for her response, surprising himself. He would make room, even if there wasn't a cabin open.

She turned to him, bewilderment on her face. "Why would you do that?" He could see the wheels spinning behind her beautiful aquamarine eyes.

"I'm not sure, to be honest with you. I've kind of shocked myself." He chuckled. "But I have never met anyone like you. And I would like to get to know you better." He paused again, focusing his eyes on hers. "Maybe we were supposed to meet."

She started to turn away but he touched her chin with his finger, bringing her face back to his. "Stay?"

"It's only Tuesday. You might change your mind before Saturday." She shook her head, and Randall realized the absurdity of his request.

He laughed, feeling careless. "I don't think so. But you can back out if you change your mind."

"I'll talk to Annie. I know she has business meetings lined up for next week, so she has to go home."

"She can stay if she wants to, but I'm inviting you." He leaned forward and spoke softly in her ear.

"Randall..."

"No expectations. Just time together. Okay?" He was probably being a fool, but he hadn't felt this way in three years.

•———————•

WEDNESDAY WAS full of activities throughout the day, but Rachel's favorite was the cowboy shootout in the afternoon. Several of the ranch's cowboys, along with others from the area, dressed in period western garb with gun belts slung low over their hips.

The cowboys shot blanks that had been loaded with black powder, and were pointed safely overhead. They were all expert gun handlers, and the result was as close to the real thing as they could get. It was loud enough, she wondered if the shots could be heard in the next town over. An authentic stagecoach rumbled through carrying a couple of women, with bandits hot on its tail. Soon there was whooping and hollering as the Cavalry arrived to stop the masked bandits and save the fair damsels that were inside.

"My hero!" One of the women actors batted her eyes at the sergeant.

"That was cheesy." Annie commented Rachel's exact thoughts and she chuckled, pointing at the younger visiting ladies who were flirting with the cowboys, taking selfies with them, and trying desperately to get their phone numbers. A couple of the cowboys even obliged, putting numbers into the girls' phones. The tall cowboy that Annie had been talking to the day before winked at her daughter. Really? Annie too? Rachel shook her head. She was not here for a fling.

Randall pulled the tall cowboy aside for a discussion, nodding at them as he did. The invitation to stay another week was tempting. But she had been burned before. And this was way too fast. They had only known each other three days. Not even that, really. What should she do?

••————————••

"YOU'RE STAYING ANOTHER WEEK?! MOM!" Annie paced across the living area.

Rachel stretched out on the couch dressed in her pajamas and fuzzy slippers. Randall had joined her for dinner again followed by another walk, this time through the stable where she admired some of the ranch's working horses. It was there, away from the other guests, that she told him she would take him up on his offer to stay another week.

"You said yourself that I needed a vacation. I'll be staying as his guest in a cabin that was not booked for next week. I guess they had a cancellation or something. And it is so peaceful here. This downtime has been good for me. So yes, I'll be staying."

"What about your flight?"

"Randall had his admin change my flight for me."

Annie raised her eyebrows. "How much did that cost?" There was curiosity in Annie's face, her eyebrows wrinkled together.

"I don't know. He wouldn't tell me. He said he gets special deals all the time."

"Um-hmm. Mom, what do you know about him? I know I joked about meeting a hot young guy, but I'm just a little worried about you."

Rachel looked heavenward as she thought. "You met him. He's. . .nice. Respectful. A complete gentleman. He must be well-off because the ranch is huge and looks financially sound. And he told me he's a widower. His wife died three years ago."

"Has he kissed you? You have come in late from your night-time strolls."

"Annie, I love that you are concerned. And no, he has not kissed me." It was much too soon to be thinking along those lines.

"He will." There was a thin smile on Annie's face, and doubt clouded her eyes. Rachel took her daughter's hands.

"It will be okay, Annie. Look, I've travelled all over the country with my project teams. I know what I'm doing. And you will just be a phone call away."

"I know. And I know this trip was my idea. But—I just don't want you to get hurt."

FOUR

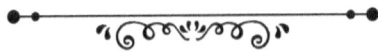

"RANDALL, is there a guest laundry around anywhere? It occurred to me that if I'm staying an extra week, I have nothing clean to wear."

"You haven't stepped in any cow patties yet, have you?"

"Um, no." Rachel giggled before scrunching her eyes together.

"Well then, don't wash your jeans just yet. They're new, right? They wear best when they've been broken in a few days." Randall chuckled at her astonished expression.

"Don't wash them? That's absurd!"

The week had flown by, and Friday came much too quickly. The week was full of activities for the guests, including a hoedown tonight. Rachel was deciding what to wear as she and Randall ate a sandwich lunch in the dining hall. Everything she had brought with her had been worn at least once.

"You are beautiful no matter what you wear. But this is a hoedown. The dress code is jeans and boots. I hope you are ready for lots of two-steppin'."

Rachel looked down at her half-eaten sandwich. "You'll

have to teach me. I watched some videos online before I came down here, but I need someone to actually walk me through it. And I'll probably step on your toes. A lot."

"I've had worse than your boots stepping on my toes. And I'll look forward to spinning you around the dance floor."

"Okay. I guess I need to get back to my room and go through my clothes one more time."

"Go ahead and pack what you don't need. The other cabin is ready for you now because the couple there left early today. I'll have one of the hands move your things as soon as they are ready."

Was she really doing this? Annie had asked her twice if she was sure about staying. But Rachel had seen her talking to the tall cowboy several times this week, leading her to believe something was going on there, too.

Rachel watched Randall finish his sandwich and take their wrappers to the garbage can. The thought of starting a new relationship, especially at her age, both frightened and excited her. But she wouldn't lay her heart on the line. It would just be another week with a nice gentleman in a peaceful setting. And yeah, she almost had herself convinced.

FRIDAY NIGHT WAS HEADY. Rachel's face was flushed from more than just dancing. Randall had barely left her side. His hands stayed at the small of her back, or around her waist, or over her shoulders, holding her hands, or somewhere on her body, and his touch was intoxicating. She moved into the cabin just before the hoedown, and Randall had shown up on her doorstep in a dazzling pearl snap shirt with embellished shoulders on the front and back. Everything on him shined from head to toe, including his eyes, which he hadn't taken off her all night.

And oh, how the man could dance. He guided her carefully and patiently through the steps before they developed a rhythm together, gliding around the floor as the band played song after song. She laughed as he twirled her out, and gasped as he twirled her in, bringing her flush against him. The twinkling lights strung around the barn blurred as he spun them together. She couldn't remember when she'd had so much fun.

After the hoedown, Randall walked Rachel to the cabin. Word had spread among the other guests that she was staying another week—without Annie—and everyone smiled knowingly when they said their goodbyes. She didn't know where this thing between her and Randall was going, if anywhere. She had been burned before. She would insist they take things slow.

They walked slowly down the path to her cabin, the waning moon lighting the way. He held her hand gently. Just enough for her to know he was there, but not so tightly that she didn't feel safe. She appreciated the gesture. They had talked some during the week about their former spouses, but neither had gone into any detail. There were still things about her ex that she wanted to keep private.

They stood outside her door and he turned her to face him.

"I'm glad you are staying an extra week. I'm really looking forward to getting to know you better."

She ducked her face shyly.

Randall lifted her chin. "You do know you're a beautiful woman, don't you?"

"You just like the rebellious blue hair." Rachel had a new twinkle in her eyes, but it was still a little uncertain.

"Well, I have to admit that was the first thing I noticed. Why do you have that, anyway?"

"I did that after my divorce. As a symbol of my independence."

"Well, that's not the only thing that attracts me to you." He shuffled his feet and took both of her hands in his. Crickets chirped. A bullfrog drummed his bass note from somewhere along the creek. A breeze ruffled through Rachel's hair. Randall closed his eyes and sighed. He looked nervous, and she wondered what he was thinking.

"Rachel, I haven't kissed a woman in three years." It was a simple statement that she knew had many layers behind it. He was still holding her hands, and his eyes were on hers, looking for her reaction.

"I haven't been kissed in . . . a long time, either." She wasn't going to admit how long it had really been.

"I haven't even looked at a woman since my wife died."

"I haven't—my husband—was a cheat. I haven't trusted anybody since then."

"You can trust me. Can I kiss you?" His eyes were bright with sincerity, his words soft.

"Can I really trust you?" She was cautious but hopeful.

"I won't hurt you, Rachel." He dropped her hands and held her face gently. She finally nodded in response and reveled in the sensation as he closed his lips over hers.

FIVE

"HOW ARE THINGS GOING, MOM?" Annie was on the West Coast meeting with a client. As an independent marketing consultant, she traveled cross-country at least once a month. Rachel was proud of her daughter and hoped that someday she would meet a good man.

"It's going well." A sigh escaped her lips before she could stop it.

"Mom? I hear a wistfulness in your voice. Are you okay?"

Annie and Rachel had had a long talk before Annie left the ranch to fly west. Rachel understood why Annie was being protective. Annie had been a victim of her father's desertion, just like Rachel had been. But she was the one who had encouraged Rachel to take the vacation in the first place.

Rachel turned on the speaker function on her phone and sat on the bed to remove her boots, thinking about how to answer. Randall had dropped her off at the cabin after another long walk around the lake. She took too long to answer.

"You aren't falling in love, are you?" The pause that followed Annie's question was loud in its silence.

Rachel switched the phone to the other hand as she slipped into her pajamas. Closing her eyes, she relived tonight's kiss in her mind. It was like the first drop of honey from the jar, full of the promise of so much more sweetness to come. And it awakened something in Rachel that she hadn't felt in ages.

"Mom?"

"I'm not here to fall in love, Annie. You know that. But he is a very nice man. . ." Her voice trailed off.

"You sound dreamy-eyed, Mom. It took an awful long time for you to answer my question. Are you sure about this? Are you getting in over your head? He hasn't cast a spell on you, has he?"

Rachel made her way to the bathroom to brush her teeth, taking her phone with her.

"I don't know. I don't think so, Annie. This is just a vacation. At the end of the week I will fly back to New York, and life will go back to normal. Well, except that I need to find a job."

"Yeah, about that. When I got home last week, there was a letter from the company that manages your IRA. It required a signature, so I signed for it."

"At least they weren't able to take that. I can't believe they committed tax fraud. Not just that. I read the CEO and CFO have been charged with money laundering, ghost employment, and embezzlement, too. It's insane. I mean, first your cheating father, and now Dencor. Why can't people just be honest?" Rachel rinsed her mouth and put her toothbrush in its plastic case.

"Is Randall honest?"

Rachel thought about that question for a moment. As far as she could tell with the way he treated his guests, he was good and true. They had gone to church together Sunday, so she knew he was a Christian. She said goodnight to Annie and pulled the covers around her. A few more days, and then she would go home. Randall would be nothing more than a memory.

•———————•

"SO, DADDY. ABOUT THIS WOMAN." Matthew had stopped Randall in the kitchen the following morning. At six-two, he was two inches taller than his father. On most things, they saw eye-to-eye. He called his father *Daddy*. It was a Texas thing. Parents were always *Daddy* and *Mama*, regardless of age. Randall appreciated the tradition, but not Matthew's reference to *this woman*.

"Her name is Rachel." Randall took a couple of pancakes off the stack sitting on the kitchen table and poured a drizzle of maple syrup over them.

"You haven't acted this way around any woman since. . ."

"Since your mother died. I know." Randall knew where this was going.

"Yeah." Matthew looked at his father quizzically. "Was it the blue stripe in her hair?"

Randall heard the tease and looked up in thought. "That definitely caught my attention. But there is something about her that just speaks to me."

Matthew raised his eyebrows. "Speaks to you? What does that mean? And now she is here another week as your guest?"

"Mmmm." Randall was enjoying his pancakes, hoping Matthew would get the message.

"Doesn't she have a job to go back to? Or a husband?"

"Divorced. Fifteen years ago."

"Family?"

"One daughter, Annie. But you know that, since you spent

an awful lot of time hanging around her last week. She's probably asking Rachel the same questions you are asking me."

"I just don't want you to get hurt, Dad." Matthew stabbed a pancake and it promptly fell off his fork.

Randall looked up, his plate already clean. "I appreciate your concern, Son. But don't you think this conversation is kind of weird? The son grilling the dad about a woman?" He grinned. "I'm fine. We don't know where this is going, if anywhere. But I feel like I'm finally living again."

"I do like seeing you happy, Daddy. But this woman. . ."

"Rachel, Son."

"Okay. Rachel. She's from New York City. As in Manhattan. Wall Street. Frou-frou coffee and mini-quiche for breakfast. Suits and ties are everyday attire. While we wear denim and chambray. Your shirts are wearing through at the elbows. Hers are, I don't know, silk or something."

"I bet she looks very nice in her wool suits and silk blouses." Randall held his empty fork in the air.

"And stiletto heels. How does a woman even walk in them, anyway?"

"What's your point, Son?" Randall pointed the fork.

"My point. . ." Matthew stabbed another pancake and finally got it to his plate. ". . .My point is that you come from two different worlds. What do you have in common?"

"You forget I sit in a corporate boardroom every quarter, surrounded by suits and ties. I know my way around that world."

"But could you live in it?"

Randall frowned.

"That's what I thought. Just be careful, please." Matthew poured a river of syrup over his stack of pancakes.

SIX

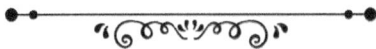

RACHEL HEARD the thud of Randall's boots on the porch of the cabin. They stopped with a pause before she heard the knock a couple of minutes later. Breathing in, then out, she stood on her side of the door, taking one more breath, before she opened it with a smile.

"Good morning, Randall."

"Good morning, Rachel. It's going to be a beautiful day. You ready for our ride?"

Randall was dressed in simple Wranglers and a chambray shirt. It looked like the one he had said was his favorite, even though it was worn in spots. Maybe he had several like that. He was a ranch owner, after all, and wore the cowboy look very, very well. In fact, everything he had on was a bit worn. Belt, boots, and hat. She was glad he hadn't decided to dress all spiffy. This was apparently his normal, everyday attire, and she liked it. Maybe one day her jeans and boots would look that comfortable.

"Let me get my hat. Then I'll be ready to play cowgirl." She smiled as she said it. She was looking forward to the full immersion experience. And spending the day with Randall.

They walked to the barn, where one of the hands had already saddled two horses for them. The scent of barn and man filled her and she inhaled deeply, making a memory of the unique combination. Horse, leather, hay, man, and even manure. She didn't think he wore any cologne, and that would make sense. It would only draw bugs. But the lovely tang called Randall Hudson drew her in like no scent ever had before.

Randall explained that he rode the same horse every day. Rocket was a Quarter Horse, tall enough that his withers stood above Rachel's eyes. His beautiful brown coat shone with obvious care, a white blaze filling his face from eyes to nose. The two of them fit together like a hand to a glove. Rocket twitched his ears and nuzzled Randall's hand in greeting. He also found the treat that Randall held out to him.

Moving to the other horse, Randall introduced her to Rachel. "This is Astro. Any time you want to ride, just let me or Matthew know and we will make sure she is saddled for you. I do ask that if I can't ride with you, that you not go alone. One of the hands can act as an escort and show you the safe areas. There are too many things that can go wrong on a ranch this size."

Rachel nodded, holding out her hand to Astro. "This is not the horse I rode last week." She admired the black coat, which was unusual for a Quarter Horse. In fact, she didn't see a speck of white or any other color anywhere on h. Astro nudged her hand, looking for a treat she knew was there. Rachel laughed at the antic.

"No. Astro is not one of the horses we use for normal guests. Those horses are bomb proof, as we say. Guaranteed to not run away. But after watching the way you handled yourself last week, and your mention that you had riding experience, I thought you might want a horse that had the energy for a great gallop across one of the fields I'm going to take you to. You ready to mount up?"

Rachel enjoyed the ride immensely. Astro was phenomenal and they bonded very quickly. Horse and rider played together on the open plain, going through paces as if they were almost dancing. They wandered through trees, crossed a couple of creeks, and finally ran across a field, laughing as they did, wild and free. They were so in tune, Rachel barely had to issue a command with her thigh or the reins, and Astro would respond immediately. She hadn't ridden like this since her twenties, and was grateful to Randall for bringing her out here, and that he would trust her with this exceptional horse.

Randall led her to another lake, one much smaller than the main eighty-acre lake. Nearby was a field of flowers that matched the color of the streak in her hair. Texas bluebonnets. She had heard of them but hadn't seen any yet, other than on the internet. This field was full of them, their heads opened up to soak in the sunshine. There must have been fifty tiny blooms on each head, the blue petals mixed with white on the top. They almost looked like they were snow-capped, but the weather was warm. There were several acres of the flowers growing wild, their heads bobbing back and forth in the breeze, welcoming her to their domain.

"This is indescribably beautiful." Rachel remained in her saddle and took in the view as Randall dismounted from his horse. She turned her head to him, seeing something in his eyes as he watched her.

"My words, exactly." His response made her blush.

Rachel finally dismounted, and they dropped their reins to the ground. Randall assured her there was no need for them to be tied. They would not move from that spot until commanded to do so. Randall pulled a picnic lunch out of his saddle bag, while Rachel pulled a checkered quilt from hers.

The cooks in the guest dining hall had prepared a simple spread of ham and cheese sandwiches, potato salad, and iced tea. Randall also carried a couple bottles of water that were infused with electrolytes, and Rachel drank one down in three long gulps. When she wiped her mouth with her sleeve, Randall laughed, bringing a guffaw from her lips and a twinkle to her eyes. *What would it be like to live with this man every day?*

Randall stood and held out his hand. "Come on. Let's go for a walk."

"Where are we going?" Rachel had on her last clean pair of jeans and a blue pullover shirt she had bought at the last minute when she did her shopping.

"We are going out to see our bluebonnet reserve."

"The field of flowers? I looked them up before coming here from New York. It is the state flower, right?"

"That's correct. We set aside a few acres designated for growing them. We don't make any money off of them, we just grow them because they are pretty. But we also don't include them in the normal guest activities because guests will want to pick them, and we want them to grow. It sounds corny, I know. It's just something we do." He picked a stem and tucked it into her hair, behind her ear. The blue petals intermingled with the blue streak, and were reflected again in the blue of her eyes.

He held both her hands and drew her closer, the look on his face spelling out his intent. Rachel let him draw her in, waiting for what would come next. When he finally dropped one hand to cup her cheek, she closed her eyes in anticipation. His kiss was soft and confident.

This man. What was she going to do?

"I have one more surprise for you today." They mounted their horses and made their way back to the barn. Randall had a gleam in his eye.

"I hope it's not dancing. This has been a great day, but I'm beat." Rachel wasn't ready for her day with Randall to end, but she hadn't spent this kind of energy in a long time and was ready to kick back with her feet up. And her legs were sore from using muscles she hadn't used in a long time.

Randall laughed. "I ride every day, and I'm still tuckered out. I was thinking more like a bowl of stew for supper, followed by a movie. If that's too much, we can hang out on the back porch of the cabin, watching for deer and listening to the crickets."

"That sounds great. A bowl of stew on the back porch, and sitting together on the swing." Randall began brushing out the horses, and Rachel picked up a brush to help.

"Why don't you go on ahead to your cabin? Rest a bit, and I'll bring the stew over in about an hour."

Rachel had to admit. She was bone-tired.

•————————•

RACHEL DIDN'T ANSWER when Randall knocked on the door of her cabin an hour later. He walked around to the back porch and found her there, asleep in one of the lounge chairs.

"Rachel." He tapped her gently on the arm. "Rachel?" She opened her eyes and blinked. "Hey, sleeping beauty. Long day, huh?"

Rachel stretched, embarrassed at having been caught asleep. "Sorry, Randall. Yes, it has been a long day, but wonderful."

"I thought for a minute I was going to have to kiss the princess to wake her up."

"Well, then, come here, prince."

She reached for him and he leaned over, placing a peck on her cheek. "Let's have some stew." He pointed to the insulated bag sitting at his feet.

They sat together at an iron dinette set that was also on the back porch. The smoky mixture of beef, vegetables, and spices warmed her, giving her just enough energy to enjoy Randall's company. He had also brought water with lemon, as well as sweet and unsweet tea. He wasn't sure what her chosen drink was. She chose the water.

When they were finished, he gathered the dishes and placed them inside the bag. He would take them to the dining room later. Taking Rachel's hand, he helped her from her chair and guided her to the swing on the other side of the porch. Drawing her close, he wrapped his arm around her.

"Listen. What do you hear?"

Rachel tilted her head in thought. "Nothing."

"I like to call that Peace and Quiet."

"It's a nice sound." They sat together as the evening sun set on the other side of the cabin.

"Rachel." He turned to face her, searching her eyes, letting his emotions show in his own. She leaned into him, saying yes with the motion, and he met her halfway.

Her lips were soft as she gave in to him. It was a slow dance of senses and emotion. Earth, wind, and fire tangled together and swirled around them. Want, need, longing, being lost, and being found.

"Wow." They both spoke at the same time, the need for air taking over. He ran his hands through her hair, the soft curls teasing him. He took her lips again in a kiss that was strong and joyful. Moving deeper, he told her things with his lips that were still too soon to say with words. Randall never wanted to look at another woman ever again. He had found the woman who could fill the empty space in his heart.

SEVEN

ON THURSDAY, Randall was busy with ranch business. Rachel took the time to read her Bible for a while, reflecting on the turn her life was taking. Was this a brief interlude? Would she go back to New York and the lifestyle she had there, putting all of this behind her? She was growing very attached to Randall. And in another life, she could have lived here and been very happy. But was this just a one-time event?

They had spent every possible moment together during the week. They had dinner at her cabin and took long walks under the Texas moon. She rode Astro out to where he was working to clear a ditch one day, taking a cowboy named Tyler with her. Digging was normally a ranch hand's job, but Randall said he still liked to get his hands dirty from time to time. When he took a break, they sat together under a nearby cottonwood tree to enjoy the lunch she had packed for them, then returned to the house together.

He did not try to "wine and dine" her, and she appreciated that, preferring instead to enjoy each other's company doing things he would do on any normal workday. Her respect for him grew, and she found herself more and more attracted to him with each passing day.

Thursday evening, Randall came to the cabin after having dinner with the guests. They sat together on the couch, watching a movie about a man who had a gift for working with skittish horses. She could easily see Randall in that role. He smelled like the outdoors. Rugged. Sunshiny. And that special scent that made him, him. She studied his jawline. Yep. Definitely movie star quality. A-list all the way.

"Whatcha thinking?" Randall had his arm around Rachel and pulled her closer.

"Just thinking how peaceful it is here. With you." She continued to study him. "And that I'm going back to New York in a couple of days. This is all going to end."

"Well, actually, I have a surprise for you."

Rachel raised her eyebrows at his statement.

"I have a meeting next week in New York with a famous steakhouse there that overlooks Times Square. We'll be talking about them using our beef." Randall held his breath while he waited for her response.

"Really? That's cool. Your beef here is excellent." She straightened to look at him more fully. "When will you be there?"

He took her hand in his, fiddling with her fingers. His hands were warm, the callouses thumping across her knuckles as he played with them. The action made her heart thump in her chest. It leapt a little higher when he kissed her hand, his lips soft and gentle against her skin.

"I fly in on Monday and meet with the owner on Tuesday. I was thinking we could spend the rest of the week together. A couple of nights on Times Square. Maybe a Broadway play." He put his arm around her shoulders again and rubbed the back of his fingers through her hair, leaning his head against hers. "We could go to the top of the Empire State Building. Make our own movie scene there." He nuzzled his nose against her neck. "And then go to your house for another day or two." Now he kissed her neck, making her shiver. "I'd love to see Annie again." His voice was soft and hopeful in her ear.

"Another week together? Isn't this moving just a little fast?" She really wanted more time with him, but her brain was saying *slow down*. And if she was being honest, a little bit of fear had crept in. But it was fear of the future—fear of being hurt—that gave her pause.

"Sweetheart, I'm fifty-five years old. Life doesn't slow down when you get to be our age. You blink and before you know it, life has moved on and you have been left behind. I'm not asking you to give me the moon, but I would like the chance to give it to you. While we have time." He turned her face to his. "Let's just see where this goes. Okay?"

Rachel swallowed. His implications were intimate. Very intimate. And as much as the thrill of being touched again in that way caused goosebumps to suddenly race down her arm, she needed to be clear about her personal boundaries. "I can't sleep with you, Randall. I have to draw the line there." She swallowed again, letting her heart lead her head. "But I would like to spend more time with you."

His grin stretched that incredible roadmap of life across his face, and he twisted her blue curl around his finger before pushing it back into place, drawing his hand along her cheek to her chin. "That's all I'm asking. Just more time. You're an incredible woman, and I don't want to think about you slipping away. Not without me."

"Okay." She closed her eyes as he placed his lips on hers. His kiss was slow and tender. Reverent, even. Her head was spinning and her heart was pounding. And she hoped she knew what she was doing.

FRIDAY NIGHT WAS the hoedown for the guests. Randall had asked Rachel to go with him, saying he didn't want to dance with anyone else. He was friendly and appreciative to all his guests, but his arm stayed around her, filling her with a warmth that kept her toes curling in her boots. She loved the faded blue chambray shirt he had on tonight. It was probably the most staple item in his wardrobe, and it fit him like a glove. And his manly ranch owner scent. Oh, my. His essence was permanently fixed in her nostrils. She knew it well and would take it back to New York with her.

They danced for hours, two-stepping and line dancing, but the slow dances were her favorite. He held her close as if they were the only two in the room, swaying with her in his arms while the band crooned tender love songs, making her weak in the knees.

She heard him chuckle in her ear, and her brain swirled as her thoughts took over.

He probably knows what kind of effect he has on me. How am I going to get through another week with him and still maintain control over my senses? I need to guard my heart.

"Randall, about next week."

"Hmmm? Hush." He placed a finger on her lips and drew her even closer. "Let's just enjoy tonight. I want every minute I can get with you before tomorrow." He danced her through the open barn door, where they swayed in the night air to the sounds of nature. And there, he kissed her soundly.

RANDALL HELD Rachel's hand as he walked her back to her cabin for the last time.

"Let's sit out here on the porch for a while and swing. For just a little bit longer."

"Okay. But I still have to get packed. You know I leave tomorrow to go home." Rachel thought about all that she had to do to get ready for her late morning flight. She didn't want to be hurrying at the last minute and leave something behind.

"That's what I want to talk about. I know I kind of sprung my meeting in New York on you. And it probably feels like a last-minute thing. But the agreement with the restaurant just came in this week. I have to think God might have had something to do with the timing. You know, giving us a little nudge to keep this thing going."

Rachel breathed in silently. "What about your ranch?"

"Matthew can handle the ranch while I'm gone. I was thinking a few days in New York could be fun. You could show me a little bit of your world."

He laid his hand next to hers, palm up, giving her the option to take it or not. She placed her fingers with his, loosely twining them together, encouraging his squeeze and slow grin.

"Look, we're not twenty-something anymore. And I'm immensely attracted to you. I thought maybe you felt the same way. Am I right?"

Rachel ducked her head, a blush spreading across her cheeks. She hoped in the moonlight he couldn't see it. "I do like you, Randall. A lot. But. . ."

"But?"

"Annie told me before we came down here that I should find some hot young guy and have a fling." She looked him square in the eye. "I don't do flings."

Randall chuckled. "Hot young guy?" He looked down at himself. "I guess one out of three isn't bad. I'm not young, and I don't know about hot, but I am a guy." He put his arm around her and pulled her close. She snuggled into him without even thinking about it. Then he tipped her chin towards him. "I'm not asking for a fling. I really do like you. Don't you want to see if there may be something more here between us? Something we can build on together?" She could see the interest in his eyes.

"Randall, it's been a long time since anyone has shown any interest in me."

"You mean the cheating louse? Rachel, I won't do that to you." He pushed the streak of blue hair away from her face.

"What about your wife? Her name was Katherine, right?" She knew his wife had died several years ago and wondered what kind of relationship they had."

"I was very much in love with Katherine. And she loved me." Randall looked away for a moment. Was he thinking back to those days? "But she would tell me it's time to move on. She would want me to be happy." He turned his face back to hers. "Don't you want to be happy?"

Rachel nodded. She really did want to be happy again. She had been pushing herself for years, staying busy, just so that she didn't slow down enough to be lonely. And if she were honest with herself, she had been lonely anyway, since Annie had become an adult with a career of her own.

"Good. Then let's see where this goes. Okay? No expectations. Just two people having fun together."

"I can do that. But I'll meet you in the city after your meeting. I need to go home and rest for a couple of days. You did keep me busy these last two weeks, you know." She grinned at him, but she was still uncertain about what they were doing. She needed some breathing room.

"Deal. I'll send my itinerary to you. I can't wait to see Times Square with you on my arm." He kissed her solidly and sweetly on the lips before pulling her closer with a little more intensity.

Rachel nodded beneath his kiss, but she needed to push him away so she could pack. "I have to go now. We will have to leave early enough to get to the airport in time for check-in and to get through security. I expect the line to be long, since it will be Saturday. Are you taking me to the airport, or is one of your ranch hands driving me over?"

"Oh, no, darlin.' That's my job. I'll meet you for breakfast and we will leave after that."

"Sounds good." Rachel sighed. Her idyllic vacation was over. She gave Randall a quick peck on the cheek. "Goodnight, Randall."

Randall kissed her back, but on the lips. "Goodnight, Rachel."

EIGHT

"YOU'RE DOING WHAT!?" Matthew looked at his dad like he had grown an extra head. The horse he was grooming looked back as Matthew tightened the cinch just a tad too tight. "Sorry, boy." He patted the gelding's rump.

"I'm going to New York. I have a meeting there on Monday."

"Is this business or pleasure? And does it have anything to do with the woman you've been googly-eyed over the past couple of weeks?"

"I'm meeting with Jolly at his restaurant about contracting to supply the beef. But I also plan to mix some pleasure in with Rachel. And yes, I will be staying at her place north of the city for a couple of days." Randall pulled a pitchfork from a tool rack and stabbed it into the ground to lean against it.

"Did she invite you, or did you invite yourself? Wait. She's a divorcee. Is she after your money?"

Randall pulled the pitchfork out of the ground and hung it back on the rack. He had a feeling this would be a difficult conversation with his son. He hadn't dated any woman since Katherine had died, and he knew that sometimes even adult kids don't want to see their parents move on.

"You don't have to be concerned for me. I'm not a teenager in puppy love. I do have a grown son, you know." He waited for that tidbit to sink in as his son smirked in return. "I invited myself, but she said yes. We're not sleeping together, and I don't think she's after my money. She has been alone for fifteen years. Don't you think that's long enough?" Randall was not shocked by Matthew's inquisition. He knew what he was doing was completely out of character for him, and he felt like he was taking a giant leap across an unknown chasm. But it was a good feeling too. Exhilarating. He hasn't felt this way since——well, since Katherine."

Matthew shook his head. "I didn't ask if you were sleeping together. That's none of my business. I'm just afraid you are suddenly biting off more than you can chew." It was an old phrase Kate used to say.

"I knew you weren't asking, but you were wondering. Weren't you?" Randall gave him that "parental" look.

"Okay, maybe I was. But I love you, Daddy. I'm glad to see you happy again, but I'm afraid you'll get hurt. You are jumping into the deep end with both feet. There might be alligators there."

Randall laughed. "I'm okay, Son. I'm really okay. And I like it."

"Well then, I'm happy for you. And I like it, too."

••———••

"MOM! What are you thinking!? I said go have a fling, not bring your fling home with you! Looks like you might have spent a lot of time riding with him, too." Annie was helping Rachel unpack. She had picked up a pair of jeans and noticed they were more worn than she expected. That wasn't Rachel's normal style.

"Yes, we did ride together. He's got a great selection of horses. Astro was wonderful. I had so much fun riding her." She took the jeans from Annie, putting them aside.

"And Randall?"

Rachel narrowed her eyes. "He's a nice, respectable man, Annie. And he's coming to New York on business first. Besides, it has been many years since I kicked your father out. I don't want to be alone anymore." Rachel didn't like being questioned like this by her daughter.

"Oh, Mom." Annie gave her a quick hug. "I don't want you to be alone either. We have each other and I'm not going anywhere."

"It's not the same, Annie, and you should be moving on, too. Meet a nice young man. Maybe that tall cowboy you spent so much time talking to. Fall in love. Get married. Give me grandbabies." There. Maybe that will turn the tables.

"Where is he staying?"

"He made a reservation at a hotel on Times Square. We'll spend a couple of days there. He wants to see the sights and maybe a play or something. Then we will come back here for a couple of days before he goes home."

"It's the 'or something' I'm worried about." Annie gave Rachel a pointed look.

Rachel laughed. "Annie, you told me to have a fling. Now you are shocked that Randall is coming to visit for a few days. But the answer to your question about the 'or something' is 'no.' If we reach that point, it will be with a ring on my finger. I'm still old-fashioned, you know."

"Oh, Mom, I love you! I just want you to be happy."

"Me too, Annie. It's time to take the leap." But would she land on solid ground, or in quicksand?

NINE

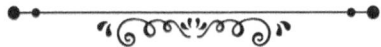

RANDALL FINISHED his business with Jolly, the steakhouse owner, at precisely three in the afternoon. Rachel was taking the train into town and was due to arrive in an hour. That gave him enough time to shed the business persona and get ready to go stepping out.

He had tickets to see *The Music Man* tonight. The story was a classic tale of the prim and proper librarian and the slick salesman who had come to town. Standing in front of the full-length mirror, he checked his appearance one more time. Dark indigo jeans, pressed and creased. Starched white button-down shirt. Gray tweed sports coat with classic western styling at the shoulders and on the sleeves. The same mother-of-pearl bolo he had worn on one of their nights together at the ranch. Finely polished ostrich skin boots and a black beaver felt Stetson. His salt-and-pepper hair had been recently trimmed, and his cheeks were nice and smooth from his visit to the professional barber in the hotel salon. No cologne. He didn't like the overpowering smell, and although she had not said anything, he got the impression that Rachel preferred him that way. It had only been a few days since he had seen her, but he couldn't wait to see her again. He nodded at the image looking back at him.

"I'm in the lobby."

His phone buzzed with her message. He would have picked her up at the station, but she insisted on taking a cab to meet him here. Since the hotel was in Times Square, they would walk to dinner and the theater from there. Leaving the room and checking to make sure the door was firmly locked behind him, he headed for the elevator, anxious for the night ahead.

Darkness fell over the city as the sun slid behind the tall buildings. Lights surrounded them as they walked. Flashing, blinking, scrolling, neon, and marquees shouting the name of the restaurant or venue they were advertising. The Tower Building at One Times Square was lit up from top to bottom with high-definition billboards playing videos, breaking news, and advertisements from retailers and other high-rolling hospitality businesses.

Randall stopped and turned to Rachel to watch the lights reflected in her eyes. She looked exquisite in a blue sweater dress that matched those eyes and fit nicely over her womanly curves. Her shoes were reasonable but elegant, a nice pump with an open toe and heel. Randall didn't know how women wore those tall spikey things. He took a deep breath and sensed something different about her. Maybe her perfume. Vanilla? Like the kitchen when Kate made cookies. Light and delictable.

"Have I told you how beautiful you look tonight?" It was cliché, but it must have been the city talking through him. This was her town. Her city. Seeing her here with him, at night, surrounded by all this man-made wonder, gave him a different view of her from what he had seen on the ranch. And she wore it well. She fit right in here, just as much as she had on the back of a horse, flying across the fields at home.

"You're looking pretty studly yourself there, cowboy." She

touched his chest with her hand before quickly removing it. "What do you think of all of this?" She waved her hand around her, gesturing toward the buildings.

"I don't see anything, darlin.' All I see is you." A different kind of stars glowed here in Times Square. They didn't compare to the stars in Texas, but his heart pounded just the same. He tipped back his hat, taking her face to kiss her softly, and she responded. The electricity flowing between them was more powerful than the millions of lights surrounding them. Taking her hand again, he fit his hat back on his head and they continued along the sidewalk, enjoying the sights and sounds of the city. Her smile was shy. His grin spread wide, like the Grand Canyon.

Dinner was at an exclusive Italian restaurant where all the pasta was made fresh to order. The portions were large, so they ordered one meal with several items, and shared it between them. Bread was constantly refilled, as was their water with lemon. Conversation was minimal between them as they ate, but it wasn't uncomfortable. Soft music played in the background, and candlelight completed the ambiance.

A waiter brought out a dessert cart full of decadent cheesecakes and other desserts. "Should we split a real New York cheesecake?" Randall wiggled his eyebrows, referring to the New Yorky cheesecake served at the ranch. Rachel sat back in her chair, her hand over her stomach.

"Oh, my. It looks incredible. But I am so stuffed, I'll probably wallow like a beached whale all night." Rachel laughed as she painted the word picture. "Of course, I may waddle like a penguin all the way to the theater."

"In that case, let's waddle." Randall chuckled as he motioned for the check, sliding his credit card to the waiter without even looking at the final cost. Rachel raised an eyebrow, but didn't comment. When the waiter returned his card and the receipt was signed, Randall stood and reached for Rachel's hand. She slid her fingers into his and he felt the softness against his own callouses, her skin warm and smooth. He was falling for her, and hoped she was doing the same.

The theater was a near-Broadway location, and the lights and signs outside were modern. But when they stepped inside the lobby, the décor looked like it may have been original to the building, which was built over a hundred years earlier. The arched ceiling was high, towering over the lobby, where stairs led to the second-floor balcony. Sconces adorned the walls every three feet, their warm yellow lights mimicking the gas lights of the era. The ceiling was the color of twilight, and small fairy lights twinkled like stars.

Inside the theater, they laughed together as the actors sang and danced through the story. Randall kept his arm around Rachel throughout the entire play. When the salesman was called out for his duplicity—since he actually knew absolutely nothing about music—Rachel muttered to herself. Randall didn't catch it all, but he thought he heard her mutter, "just like my husband." He squeezed her shoulders to comfort her. He would never treat her that way.

They walked back to the hotel, where Randall had booked connecting rooms. Saying goodnight, he kissed her before leaving her at her door. Matthew and Annie had both expressed their concerns, and he wanted to make sure there was no hint that he was anything less than a gentleman.

•—————••

RACHEL FLOPPED down on the softest bed she had ever slept in, reflecting on her date with Randall. It was too late to call Annie, and she wanted to simply bask in the glow of her time with the incredibly handsome man. He had put her first in everything tonight, always touching her back, holding her hand, or placing his arm around her shoulder. It kept the connection sizzling between them, and she almost wished there wasn't a locked door between their rooms. But she had set her boundaries, and he had honored them. It made her even more attracted to him.

Randall had kissed her right there on the sidewalk. In front of everybody. It was only a moment, but it was a magical moment. In the few short years that she and Annie's father had been married, he had not brought her to Times Square a single time, and had never kissed her in such a public place.

The play was fun, but the story reminded her of how she had already been swindled. First, by her ex-husband who had cheated on her more times during their ten-year marriage than she wanted to acknowledge. Then there was Dencor, which had been raided by the FBI for fraud. They hadn't cheated *her*, per se, but in the course of committing fraud they had cheated their customers and their employees.

But Randall was different. Honorable to the core. They had only known each other for a little more than two weeks, but she believed she could trust him completely. He would never do anything to deceive her.

She finally changed into her pajamas and slipped between the thousand-count cotton sheets, welcoming the dreams she knew she would have tonight. Tomorrow would be a full day of sightseeing and she needed to be fully rested.

TEN

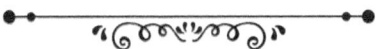

THEY SPENT all of Wednesday seeing various sights in the city. They made the obligatory tourist ferry ride to the Statue of Liberty, where they could look back on the New York skyline, enjoying lunch at a small deli there. They visited the New York Public Library, the Chrysler Building, and Hell's Kitchen, where they walked along the sidewalk enjoying the aromas coming from the various restaurants. They also visited the 9/11 Memorial. The reverent quiet surrounded them, and Randall wished they had scheduled more time there.

Night was falling as they reached their last stop at the Empire State Building. Randall had purchased an express pass to take them to the top observation deck. By this time, the sun was sliding once again behind the buildings. They walked all the way around the four sides, where they were able to see the aerial view of the same sights they had seen from the ground.

Randall kept his hand on Rachel's back as they roamed around the deck. The sights were breathtaking, but not as much as his view of Rachel as she oohed and awed over the scenery. Even though this was her city, she had told him she had not visited most of the iconic attractions. He was glad he had chosen to do this.

"I'd love to know what you're thinking." He held his arms around her from behind. She leaned back against him and he soaked in her sweet scent, wrapping her in his warmth.

"I just realized something. I've lived in New York for over half my life, but I have never seen anything like this." She turned in his arms to face him. "My world is so vastly different from yours. And as marvelous as all of this is, it doesn't compare to clear skies and stars shining overhead. I'd give up the traffic, noise, and busyness for cattle mooing and crickets chirping any day, if I could.

Randall tucked her head under his chin and held her there. What if he could talk her into moving to Texas?

••————————••

RACHEL TOOK in the view from the top observation deck of one of the tallest buildings in the city. She was slightly dizzy, but she wasn't sure if that feeling was because of the height—one hundred and two stories above the city—or because of the man who now held his arms around her. It was much too soon for these thoughts, but she couldn't help but wonder what it would be like to be married to Randall Hudson. Right now, he was kind, considerate, and attentive, making sure to go the places she wanted to go. His hand was always at her back in a protective way. His smile was always mirrored in his eyes, and those beautiful brown orbs were always directed toward her, not looking off over her shoulder or to her side.

Through the past years she had intentionally stayed single, not wanting to put her heart on the line again. So she had poured her energy into seeing Annie through college as well as building a career for herself. Then her life had turned upside down once again when she lost her job. Was Randall her future?

When Rachel made the decision to stay an extra week with him in Texas, Annie told Rachel to guard her heart. Now here she was, seeing all the best sights in the city she had lived and worked in for years, but had never enjoyed. And it was all due to the man who had shown her the finest in Texas hospitality right here in New York City. Tomorrow, they would travel back to her home just north of the city, where he would stay another two days before heading back to Texas. They didn't have anything specific planned. It would simply be time together.

⸻

THE NEXT DAY, they ate a late breakfast in the hotel restaurant before taking a cab to Grand Central Station. They could have taken their cab to their suburb north of the city, but in order to give Randall the full experience of Rachel's work life, they took the train. An hour later, they arrived at her home. Annie was working from home today and had promised to put a roast and veggies in the slow cooker, so that it would be ready by the time they rolled in. Would they get along? What would she do if Annie rejected the idea of Randall in her life?

"Mom! You're home!" Annie ran down the steps from the porch to the driveway as Randall paid the driver and retrieved their luggage. Rachel hugged Annie tight, surprised at her exuberant greeting. She turned to Randall, who had joined them after the cab driver pulled away, and wrapped her hand around his arm.

"Hello, Randall. Welcome to New York." Annie was gracious, as always. Rachel relaxed.

Randall gave Annie's hand a firm squeeze. "It's a pleasure to see you again, Annie. With those lovely blue eyes, you two could be twins." His own brown eyes twinkled.

Annie looked at Rachel with a pointed glance and said, "He's a smooth talker, Mom." Turning to Randall, she responded to his greeting with a smile. "Come on in. I've got a room set up for you. You can drop your luggage in there." Turning back to Rachel, she continued, "I put him in the last room on the left side of the house." The smirk on Annie's face told Rachel what Annie was thinking. Rachel's room was on the far end of the right side. The house had two wings, with the kitchen and family room in the middle. Annie's room was on the right side, between them.

"We don't need a chaperone, daughter." Rachel raised one eyebrow.

"Just doing for you, what you would do for me." Annie's face held another smirk and she turned away, leaving them alone.

•————————•

RANDALL ENJOYED a pleasant evening with Rachel and Annie, who entertained both of them with tales of working with some of her clients. Most claimed they were technically savvy, but when it came to digital marketing, they didn't know where to start. Annie did most of her work remotely, meeting with her clients via internet sessions. But she also travelled from time to time, especially when the client was high-profile.

It became apparent that Rachel's life here in New York was far different than his in Texas. How hard would it be on a relationship between them? The chemistry between them made his heart zing, but his life and his livelihood were both in Texas.

He could not pack up his ranch and move it. On the other hand, Rachel was now unemployed. Would she consider relocating?

After breakfast the next day, Rachel took Randall to a waterside park on the Hudson River. While her neighborhood was tree-lined, the houses were close together, and privacy was at a premium. They picnicked by the river, watching the barges glide through the water on their way to deliver whatever product they carried. It was a peaceful way to spend the day. But his focus was still on Rachel.

"You have a beautiful town to live in. How large is it?" Randall stretched out his legs to relax on the blanket they had spread on the riverbank.

"It is technically a village, although we do have a major. I think it's about three or four square miles, or something like that. It's just big enough, close enough to the city, but also far enough away. A nice compromise." Rachel put the chicken salad back into the cooler and pulled out the small tarts she had picked up for dessert.

"Hm." Randall did a quick search on his phone. The Double H was ten times larger than Rachel's entire town. Yet there were over three thousand homes crowded together here. Surely, he could woo Rachel away from that. He began to develop a plan in his mind.

"Pie?" Rachel handed him one of the tarts.

"Mmm. Peach. One of my favorites." He smiled his most effective smile. It had been a long time since he had courted a woman, but that was what he planned to do.

Their picnic was nice, and the park was well maintained. But he missed the sounds and smells of blue skies, grass waving naturally in the fields, cows munching, the occasional horse's whinny, and the beautiful bluebonnets that were the color of Rachel's eyes.

They watched the barges cruise up and down the river, along with the recreational boats that floated outside the shipping lanes. It was an idyllic scene. But it was not home.

A few ideas began to churn in his mind. How to convince Rachel to leave New York was number one. Once he had achieved that goal, there would be a matter of housing in Texas, although he was more than happy to offer one of the cabins to her and Annie. He didn't know what Rachel's finances were like, especially since she was now unemployed, but he could help with moving expenses. If she would accept the help. He didn't want to insult her, and it would be a fine line to walk.

ELEVEN

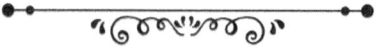

"SO, Rachel. We have all of today to spend together." Randall poured the natural maple syrup over the waffles that Rachel had made for breakfast. "Then I go home tomorrow. What do you want to do today?"

"Let's just hang out together here. Maybe you can help me decide what I need to do next. I need to start job hunting. In fact, I should have been doing that instead of taking a vacation for the past three weeks." She set another plate of waffles on the table, grinning at the man who had already devoured his first plate full. He had a contemplative look on his face.

"What kind of job are you interested in? You were a program manager with Dencor, right? That should translate well to similar positions in other companies."

"That might be true, except that I'm not sure I want to travel as much as I did before. Most of the people on my project teams were young enough to be my kids. And they were beginning to run circles around me."

"But that was their job, right?" Randall leaned his face into his hand, one finger tapping his magnificent jawline. "Your job was to make sure that they completed their tasks on time, keeping the projects on track."

"And under budget. Senior management was always concerned about budget."

"And now there is no senior management because there is no company. It was fraud, right? Do you know what they did that caused the charges?"

"No. It had to all have been at levels way over my head. At least I know I am innocent. But think of the impact to all of the employees who are now also job hunting, like me. And I'll be competing against all of them. Experience doesn't mean much these days. Too much experience on a resume indicates age. And let's be honest. Age discrimination exists. They just paint it a different color, calling it 'overqualified'." Rachel pushed her plate back. She was suddenly not very hungry.

"Do you have to stay in New York?" Randall began clearing the table, his face blank.

"I don't know where else I would go." She felt so forlorn. She turned her head to the side, not wanting him to see the tears that were building.

"Well, let's clear these dishes. I'd like to take you to dinner and a movie this afternoon. How about it?"

"That's fine. In fact, that would be wonderful. It is your last night here, after all. Tomorrow, we both go back to the real world. You, to your ranch. And me—to——I'm not sure yet." *What am I going to do?*

•——————•

THE MOVIE WAS A SUSPENSE THRILLER. Randall hoped it would distract Rachel enough that she would not worry about her future for one more night. But he spent the time mulling over ideas in his head. She tugged at his heart in a way that no woman had since his wife, Katherine. He wanted to hold her. To protect her. To replace the worry with a goal. He wanted to make her happy. But there was over eighteen hundred miles between them. It would be hard to maintain a relationship with that kind of physical distance.

It was late when they returned to Rachel's home. Randall took her hand and led her to her back porch, and the glider he had noticed yesterday. A crescent moon hung just low enough to still be seen before dipping beyond the horizon. He sat down beside her, wrapping his arm around her shoulders and pulling her close. He kissed her temple, trying to build up his courage before making his next suggestion. They sat in silence for a while.

When Rachel laid her head on his shoulder, the action gave him the courage to share his idea.

"Come to Texas with me."

He hadn't intended to spill the words like that, but they were out now.

"What? I can't just up and move." Rachel lifted her head and turned to face him, her brow furrowed, a look of shock on her face.

"Sure, you can. What's keeping you here?" He knew he was being blunt and should have eased into this discussion, but it was too late now. "Come on. I can make you happy." He rubbed her lip with his thumb and kissed the corner of her mouth.

"Randall, stop, please. Let me think." She pushed him away. "Annie lives here. I can't just move away from her."

"Annie's a big girl." He turned her sideways and pulled her legs across his lap.

"What about the house? I still have a few years left on the mortgage."

"Sell the house."

"I can't do that. Where will Annie go?" Rachel pulled her legs off his lap and turned to face him fully.

"I'll buy her a condo." He was all in now. Deep waters, with no waders. He might even need scuba gear at this point.

"Be reasonable." She stood.

"I am completely serious. We click, Rachel. You and me. You know we do. I know it seems fast, but I have fallen head over heels for you. Come to Texas. Please." Randall stood also and took both hands, pleading.

"I don't know. Maybe we should slow down." Rachel was a planner. Methodical. The past three weeks had been outside her comfort zone, and Randall could see that she was pulling back.

He sat down again on the glider and pulled her close beside him, kissing her temple. He really wanted to do a little last-night-in-New-York necking. "I was thinking something different. I've never met anyone like you. You excite me. Talk to Annie. Please. She'll understand." He took a deep breath, feeling like he was running out of time. "Maybe you just put the house on the market, and see what happens." He held her face between his hands, searching her eyes, before taking her lips with his.

"Mom, can I see you in the kitchen, please?" Annie's voice came from the back door.

Randall ducked his head, then stood up. "I guess that's my cue." His time was up.

Rachel sighed. "I guess so." She stood with him.

"Rachel, this was not a fling for me. I'm wanting long term. Talk to Annie. I'll see you in the morning." He kissed her one last time—long enough to make his meaning clear.

• •——————• •

"TALK TO ME ABOUT WHAT?" Annie pulled Rachel into the kitchen as Randall made his way to his room.

"You just said you wanted to talk to me, Annie. What's up?" Rachel did her best to sound nonchalant.

"What's up? What's up with you and Randall? It sounded like an argument out there." Annie walked around the island, reminding Rachel of a scolding parent.

"He wants me to move to Texas." Rachel watched Annie's face for her reaction.

Annie froze. "Is it that serious, Mom?"

Rachel shook her head. "I don't know. He wants me to sell the house."

"Sell the house?" Annie raised her eyebrows.

"He said he would buy you a condo. Can you believe that?"

"Mom, I don't know about this. And I don't want him to buy me anything." Annie folded her arms, her mouth in a thin line of determination.

"I know, Annie. But I really like him. I think he may be the one." And Rachel felt like a teenager, with the age-old angst, *"You don't understand."*

Annie tapped her fingernails on the granite countertop. Rachel had that put in after she and Annie's father bought the house. "Have you prayed about it? I mean, I know we haven't gone to church in a long time. But sometimes, if I'm trying to make a decision, I talk to God about it."

"No. Randall just now brought it up. I haven't had time to think it through. But maybe it is time to move on and build a new life. It appears that my life here may be dead now, anyway."

"Well, pray about it. Maybe. . ." Annie put her hand on her

chin in thought. "Maybe you should put the house up for sale. If it sells, that's God's answer. And if it doesn't sell, well, that's your answer too."

Rachel picked up her Bible later that night, not really searching for an answer, but yet hoping God would send her a message. An email would be nice. Text message. Something loud and clear that would say *"move"*. She was terrified and excited at the same time. But she knew she shouldn't take this decision lightly. She would be picking up her entire life—and Annie's—to move to a new state and possibly pursue a new relationship with Randall.

She hadn't dated anybody since her divorce. No one. It was really nice spending time with Randall and letting him pamper her. But that wasn't sustainable. There had to be a more solid foundation, didn't there? How would they build on the whirlwind of the last three weeks?

She had laid her Bible down without looking at it, and now her eyes fell to where it had opened in Genesis.

"The Lord had said to Abram, 'Go from your country, your people and your father's household to the land I will show you.'"

Her Bible was old, given to her by her mother when she was thirteen. She looked up the verse online, in several versions, wondering if she was reading it wrong. But she wasn't. It very clearly held instructions to Abraham to move. And God didn't even tell him where. It was kind of like one of those I'll-tell-you-when-you-get-there situations. Just trust. Well, hadn't she just said to herself that she wanted a message that said "move"? And here it was, in black and white. She would talk to Annie tomorrow after Randall left for the airport. She didn't want him to be included in that conversation. It would need to be kept solely between herself and Annie.

TWELVE

"WHERE HAVE YOU BEEN, Randall? We haven't seen you in weeks." The guys at the Table of Knowledge all looked at each other with smirks on their faces. Their waitress made the rounds with more coffee, then set the pot in the middle of the table.

"Ranch business." He sat in the one remaining chair and poured his own cup.

"Would that business happen to involve a woman with blue hair?" Earl nudged Randall with his elbow.

"Her hair's not blue." He took a sip and realized his mistake as the guys guffawed.

"Humf! So there is a woman. And we know all about her too. One of your fancy New York guests." Ned challenged Randall with his eyes.

"I did meet a woman, yes." Maybe he should have stayed home today.

"And she stayed an extra week."

"Yes, but she is back home in New York now." He motioned to the waitress and ordered pancakes.

"So where were you last week then?" Ned wiggled his eyebrows. He was being a pest.

"I went out of town on business. Got a new contract to supply beef to an upscale restaurant."

"And where is this restaurant?" Harris asked this question. He was usually quiet.

"You know good and well where it is." They all laughed heartily.

"Didn't one of you guys wrestle an alligator last week?" That story never failed to deflect whatever conversation was going on. That tiny little gator grew bigger every time Ned told the story, like he had just tussled with the thing yesterday.

"No, no, no." Earl smiled. "You're not gettin' away with that this time. Come on now. We want all the details."

"Here ya are, sugar." The waitress set the pancakes down in front of him with a wink.

Had she been listening? Of course she had. This was the Table of Knowledge, where all things in Nora Hills were discussed by those who held court here. But Randall didn't like being in the hot seat. He poured a generous serving of syrup over the stack and took a bite. He would give them just enough information to satisfy their curiosity for now. But even he didn't know where this thing with Rachel was going. If it was going anywhere.

•——————•

TWO WEEKS PASSED with no word from Rachel. He had texted her a couple of times just to check in, but she hadn't answered. Randall was beginning to think he had imagined the connection between them. Or maybe he was jumping the gun himself. Was he ready for a new relationship? Not too long ago, he had told the guys at the restaurant he didn't need a new woman. He was content. Settled.

Annie and Matthew had exchanged messages a few times, but Matthew hadn't shared any details, other than to say Rachel was still in New York while Annie was visiting clients.

He hated waiting. He was a take-action kind of guy.

Out in a back pasture, he watched his cattle graze on the sweet Bermuda grass. He sat easily on Rocket, his mind whirling with thoughts of the past month. Rachel had come and gone like a sand tornado. Some called the giant swirls of sand a dust devil, but Rachel was no devil. She was, however, a tornado, in and out of his life so fast it left him wondering what had happened. Had those three weeks even been real? Or was it really just a fling?

He jumped when the phone rang, cutting through his thoughts. Rachel's name and picture popped up on his screen.

"Hi, Randall." She stopped, her voice hesitant.

"Hello, Rachel. I was beginning to thing you were a figment of my imagination."

"Yeah, um, I've been busy with getting the house on the market. And guess what? I have received three offers, and it has only been on the market four days! Is that crazy?"

Randall blew a sigh of relief, while Rocket snorted. He took another deep breath. In, and out.

"Three offers? That's fantastic." Randall shifted in the saddle. "Are they good offers?"

"One is ten thousand below asking, so that one is out already. The other two are over asking price. Twenty thousand, and fifty thousand!"

"Fifty thousand over asking? Well, you obviously want to accept that offer, right?"

"That one is from a vacation rental company. They say they have a family from Japan that wants to rent the house long term—like four or five years—while their daughter is studying at NYU."

"Well, that sounds like a good reason to sell to them."

"But the other offer is a young family with two small kids. You should see them. They sent a picture with the offer. They are so cute, and they wrote the best letter saying how much they want to raise their kids here. It was so sweet."

"So you take that offer, instead. I don't understand the problem." It seemed simple, to him.

"Oh, I don't know, Randall. It is all happening so fast. The vacation rental offer includes the furnishings. That leaves me with nothing. Nothing! I would have to start completely over."

"You can counter-offer. Select the pieces you want to keep and write that into the counter."

Rachel sighed. "I don't think I'm ready for this."

Randall tried not to panic. "Didn't you say that this would be a test to find out what God wanted you to do? You said if the house sells, it was your confirmation that you should move here with me. And you have two solid offers on the table."

"I don't know. . ."

"Rachel, I really like you a lot. I think we would be great together. I'm committed. If that is what is holding you back, you don't have to worry."

"This just seems like an awful lot of change in a very short time. I'm more methodical than that. I need to see and weigh all the evidence before picking up my life and moving it across the country. And I need to talk to Annie. She lives here too. I'll let you know what I decide."

"OKAY, Mom. You've done plenty of cost-benefit analysis in your job. Let's look at the pros and cons." She opened her laptop. "I'll make a list.

PROS—Fifty thousand over asking. And you don't have to move your furniture unless you decide to keep some."

"What if I take the other offer?"

"That would be one pro and two cons. Less money, and higher moving costs." Annie made her notes.

"Other CONS—you need to find a new house."

"Randall said we could stay in one of his cabins until we found something."

"Okay. Erase that con. But another con is if you don't sell. You are stuck here with no job and no income."

"I do need to find a job, wherever I go. And if I move to Texas, I don't know anyone who could help me make connections."

"Except Randall."

"Well, yes. But he hasn't said anything about helping with that. And I don't want to be beholden to him any more than I already am." Rachel tapped her fingernails on the table. Maybe she should splurge and get a manicure. It had been a while.

"Beholden? Mom, who uses that word anymore?"

"Stick to the topic. What about you? I don't want to disrupt your life." She twisted her blue curl. It was starting to come in gray. That would have to be done soon, too.

"I'm in digital marketing. I can work from anywhere."

"All right. That's a pro then. So what do you think, Annie?"

"It doesn't matter what I think. This is your house. Your life. Your decision whether or not you move, with or without Randall. And how do you feel about him? Do you trust him?" She leveled her eyes at Rachel. She really would make a great parent someday.

"Mom." Her daughter softened her tone. "You have been alone for fifteen years. If something happens to me. . ."

"Like if you meet someone and fall in love? I don't want to talk about anything bad happening, but you deserve a future of your own." Rachel was starting to see the picture.

"Exactly. I don't want you to be alone. I know you're independent, but don't you think it is time to let somebody love you?" Annie held Rachel's hand in hers, a mixed look of love, protection, and pleading in her eyes. "You know I have reservations about Randall. But I think it's time for a new adventure. God plunked His answer right into your lap. And I will be there with you."

Rachel hugged Annie tightly. Her daughter was never afraid to speak her mind, and this time she was right. "Okay, then. I'll call the realtor in the morning and accept the offer from the vacation rental company." She blew out a breath. It felt good to make a final decision. "Oh, Annie! I'm actually excited!"

In the end, she decided to start over with a clean slate. She didn't want any items left over from her failed marriage as reminders of what had been. When they got to Texas, it would be with a full bank account and a list of realtors and furniture stores. It was still nerve-wracking, but her life had turned a significant corner with the loss of her job. Why not start completely over? And with a handsome cowboy, as well?

They sorted through their clothes again, deciding to give their heavy winter items to a local charity for the homeless. Linens, dishes, pots and pans—it all went to the charity.

Rachel slumped onto the foot of her bed, looking around at all the boxes. This was her life. Three decades of memories, all stuffed into packing crates to give away. They had kept their pictures. Annie wanted those, and Rachel understood why. Was she making a mistake by erasing all the memories completely? What if things went south with Randall? She laughed nervously at her own pun. She was actually moving south.

She walked into the bedroom that she had used as her office. Most of her files had been shredded, with the exception of anything related to the house. Opening the large envelope that sat on the desk, she found the marriage certificate and the divorce decree. The beginning of her marriage, and the end of it. No regrets. This was part of the journey she had taken called life. She had Annie as a result, and she had proven her ability to take care of herself. She didn't need a man's help. Before she zipped her carry-on suitcase, she tucked the envelope into an inside pocket. It was time to go.

THIRTEEN

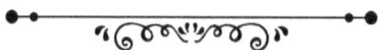

RACHEL SIGHED as Randall pulled the SUV under the large archway with the Double H Ranch words built into the wrought iron. They were entering the family side, away from the resort side where she and Annie had stayed the first week, and she stayed the second week. She was excited and nervous at the same time, and glanced back at Annie, who sat up as soon as they reached the ranch. Her eyes roamed, taking in the broad expanse of land. This would be their new home until they found another place to live.

"Welcome to the Double H. I am so glad you decided to stay here with us for a while." Randall had tipped his sunglasses down to look at Annie through the rear-view mirror.

"I appreciate the offer, Randall. I have to admit it is a little daunting to move to a new state and start over, even though I still have my same job. And I'm looking forward to seeing the rest of the ranch. This is incredible." Annie's eyes gleamed with excitement.

Rachel marveled at the various buildings as they drove past

them on their way to the cabin. The main homestead sat on a slight hill that overlooked the ranch behind it. The guest house was around the corner in a more secluded spot, with the cabins beyond. Barns and stables were situated farther down a gravel road.

"How many acres do you have here, Randall? I know you mentioned it on the trail ride, but I don't remember." Rachel turned her head each way.

"We have twenty-five thousand acres. That's over thirty-nine square miles."

"Many times larger than our entire suburb back in New York." Annie chimed in.

"Did you build all of this yourself, Randall? Or is it family land?" Rachel had read that most large ranches had been handed down from father to son for several generations.

"About half of the land was passed down from my great-grandfather. The rest has been acquired by the ranch over the years."

"Acquired by the ranch? I don't understand."

"The ranch is incorporated. Any new land or major assets become property of the corporation."

Rachel raised an eyebrow. This was new information.

They drove through the ranch to the resort. Randall stopped the SUV in the guest parking lot, which was close to the cabins. "Here we are. Home sweet home. Leave your bags in the car. I'll have one of the ranch hands take them in for you."

Rachel stepped through the doorway as Randall held it open for them. She took a deep breath. The scent of clean air, the trees along the creek bank, horse, cow, and other ranch smells lingering lightly in the cabin. And on the man beside her.

This cabin was larger than the one she had stayed in a few weeks ago. It had an open living area that included the kitchen, dining area, and a set of soft leather furniture placed in front of a stone fireplace. It was not a gas fireplace. She would have to learn how to build a fire the old-fashioned way. Maybe Randall would show her how to do that.

"The kitchen is fully stocked. I had groceries delivered for the fridge and pantry this morning. You shouldn't have to shop for anything. But you can feel free to dine with the guests anytime you want to, as well. I've already informed the staff there that you have carte blanche.

Rachel looked at Annie, her eyes opened wide. This was much more than either of them had expected. Too much, really.

"That's not necessary, Randall, but thank you for the offer. We can cook, you know." Rachel smiled at him, not wanting to start off with any tension between them. But it was a little unnerving that he had taken the liberty to set everything up for them.

Randall placed his hand on Rachel's back and escorted them to the rear of the cabin, where they found two bedrooms, each with its own bathroom. The décor was homey, with queen beds, cedar furniture, and a large television in each room.

"What about our cars? Do you know when they will be delivered? And thank you so much for having them shipped. It would have been a long drive, otherwise." Randall had also purchased first-class seats for their flight from New York. Another point she had taken exception with.

"They will be here later this week. You can use the SUV we drove from the airport, in the meantime. I'll leave the keys on the hook by the front door. It belongs to the ranch fleet, so you can use it any time."

Rachel turned to Randall, one hand on her chest. "Thank you so much. For all of this. I'm overwhelmed."

Randall pulled her into his arms and tilted her face toward his.

"I hope I haven't overstepped. But when I didn't hear from you for two weeks, I was afraid I might have pushed you too far. I know this is fast, but I don't need to guess about what our future might look like. I want you in it. That's all I need to know. And I've waited weeks to do this."

His kiss was soft and gentle, and Rachel enjoyed it. But she still had doubts and pushed him away.

"I had to think. I'm a planner, you know. But after I called the realtor, everything fell into place so quickly it seemed like it was God telling me to get up and go. But if I'm honest, I'm still scared."

"I'll take care of you, Rachel." Randall's words were warm and inviting.

"That's just it, Randall. I don't want you to take care of me. I've been on my own for a long time. I need to do this my way."

⸳———⸳

THE SUN SHONE in a cloudless April sky as Rachel drove through town, becoming more familiar with the types of businesses and possibilities for employment. Most of them were supportive of the area ranchers. There was the Farm and Ranch Store, two different feed mills, a big box lumber yard, and a smaller lumber mill. Grocery stores, big box chain stores, a hardware store, a smattering of restaurants, and a few Mom and Pop places rounded out the possibilities.

The square was the beehive for the Mom and Pop stores. A

donut shop, a bookstore, an antiques store, a coffee shop, two banks, and the courthouse.

None of them would offer the same pay scale she was used to as a program manager for a large Manhattan firm. A firm that no longer existed.

There was also the school. But she could not teach without the required state certificate. Maybe a local ranch would hire her. Then again, Randall would not want her to work for anyone else.

That brought up the most pressing question. What was she going to do about him? He had pried her away from New York and swooshed her over a thousand miles away. Picked her and Annie up in a whirlwind, like the dust devils she had seen in videos on the internet. Annie had settled in nicely, making quick friends with Matthew.

Was she ready to love again? Did she even want to try? Or was her heart already gone?

Needing relief from her search, she stopped by Debbie's Restaurant. Ordering a salad, she reflected as she munched. She really enjoyed Randall's company. And oh, his kisses. But where was her life headed? Was there truly a future for them, or was this all a fairy tale?

•———————•

RACHEL LOOKED around as she walked into Debbie's Restaurant the next day. It was early in the morning. Randall had a meeting somewhere, and she had heard him talking to Matthew one day about coming here for breakfast. Her salad yesterday was good, so she decided to try out the breakfast, but when Randall wasn't here.

"Whoo-wee!" Rachel turned at the sharp sound.

"Lookee there! Is that Randall's gal?"

"Hush! She can probably hear ya."

A round table sat in a corner to her left. Four older men sat around it, with two empty chairs. Over the table hung the sign she had heard about. "Table of Knowledge."

One of the men was a bit younger—closer to her age. He stood and approached her with his hand out.

"I am so sorry. My friends are a bit uncouth. I'm Mike. And you must be Rachel."

Rachel ignored the man's hand. Coming here was a mistake. She started back toward the door, but Mike stopped her with a soft touch on her arm.

"Please. Let me apologize. Would you like some coffee? I'll buy."

Rachel followed Mike to the table while three sets of eyes watched. The waitress met her with a cup of coffee, three creamers, and a blueberry muffin. *How did she know?*

"Randall says you like your cream with a little coffee." The oldest man smiled. "I'm Harris. And these idiots are Earl and Ned."

"I'm Rachel. But I guess you already know that. Randall's been talking about me?"

"He's smitten."

"Cain't talk about nothing else. Rachel this, and Rachel that."

Rachel poured all three creamers in her coffee and stirred before taking a sip. *Perfect.*

"I can see why he likes you." Harris ribbed Earl with his elbow.

"Why is that?" This is why she came. *If you want to know about the man—talk to his friends.* That's what her mother used to say.

"You've got class."

Rachel raised an eyebrow, and Harris continued.

"You're eatin' your muffin with a fork. Ned, here, don't even know what a fork is."

They all laughed, and Rachel decided she liked them. They would be a great source of information about the man who had captured her attention.

FOURTEEN

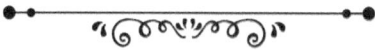

RANDALL DIPPED his toast into the yolk of his over-easy eggs and took a large bite, using his napkin to catch the drips. His father had called them dippin' eggs, and they were his favorite breakfast meal. He had inherited that taste and had their cook fix them at least once a week.

"Matthew, we are expecting the new horse today. I'd like to keep the delivery under wraps for now. That means from our guests—and I do mean all of our guests."

"So hide the delivery from Rachel and Annie? How should we do that?" Matthew took his own bite of eggs. "Maybe you can distract them." His eyebrows wiggled with the implication.

"No, I need to be here for this delivery. The truck will come in through the back side of the ranch, and the horse will be housed in the second stable, with the private stall. We'll leave him there while we have him checked out by the vet, and also give him a chance to settle in before we turn him out into the pasture."

"Is there a reason you don't want Rachel to know about him?" Matthew's face showed concern.

"I have a plan for him, and Rachel is part of that plan. But I want it to be a surprise. So mum's the word."

"Gotcha. But, Daddy, I think you've gone plumb crazy."

Randall thought he might be a bit crazy, too, but not because of the horse. It was a good investment, whether Rachel liked it or not. No, he was crazy for Rachel, and he couldn't stop himself from thinking about her. She was not far away, in the cabin he had set aside for her and her daughter. He wondered what they had fixed for breakfast, or was she even up yet? It was early—just after six in the morning. Does she sleep well? Is the bed comfortable enough? Does she wear sweats and a T-shirt? Flannel pajamas? Or something soft and pretty? And why do men always ask that question? She would look good in anything.

She and Annie had been here three weeks, and Randall's days were so busy he had barely had time to see her. But he did allow his mind to wander and plan. What would those blue eyes think about driving into San Antonio for a weekend? They could take a walk along the river. Or maybe he could ask Matthew to do something with Annie, so he and Rachel could have time alone together. Yeah. That's a better idea. He would have Matthew distract Annie, so he could keep Rachel company at the cabin. They could cook dinner together. Watch a movie while cuddled under a blanket on the sofa. He would play with the blue curl that falls over her forehead. Maybe a little sparkin.' That's a term he had heard his grandfather use. And sparkin' seemed an appropriate word. There certainly was a current between them.

"Daddy? You done with your plate?" Matthew nudged him on his shoulder, a smirk on his face.

"Hm? Oh. Yeah. I'm done." Or maybe I'm just getting started. He refocused. He had a horse being delivered today.

RACHEL DRESSED in her jeans and boots, which were starting to become much more comfortable, just as Randall said they would. He was taking her riding again today, and she was looking forward to racing across the field on Astro.

Annie was out looking at condos. She said she wanted to buy her own space, but she would look at two bedrooms so that Rachel could move in if she wanted to. They had been in Texas three weeks, and Annie wanted to be closer to town. She also said she felt like she was taking advantage of Randall's hospitality, and she wasn't comfortable with that. She hoped to find a place with a great location and quick closing.

Rachel suspected that Annie felt like a fifth wheel. There was no privacy for the two of them here in the cabin. Actually, that didn't bother Rachel. It meant they had to slow down and let the relationship build, rather than flaring into a hot fire that would sizzle for a while, but flame out when they got bored with each other.

Randall had joined the two of them a few nights for dinner. And Matthew had invited Annie to a baseball game one night. Turned out that Matthew was the tall cowboy Annie spent so much time talking to during their first week at the resort. Rachel suspected the invitation was to give herself and Randall space, but she also thought it was good for Annie to get out and meet people her own age. The move had disrupted her life, too.

A knock at the door announced Randall's arrival at the cabin. She must have been daydreaming. She usually heard his boots on the porch first. Throwing open the door, she admired his handsome profile. He was looking off to one side, where something had caught his attention.

"Hey, Randall. I'm ready to ride."

His warm brown eyes skimmed over her, curls to boots and back again, a slow smile creating that map of wrinkles that she loved so much. Experience lived on his face, touched by hope and expectation. He held out his hand to take hers.

"Your carriage awaits, M'lady. I've got a surprise for you." He wiggled his eyebrows, his Texas twang coming through his attempted English accent.

Randall had already given her several small surprises since she moved to the ranch, not to mention her second week as his guest and his following trip to New York. He had brought the ATV, which meant they must be going somewhere farther than walking distance.

"I thought we were going to ride today." It was sunny and not too hot, which made a perfect day to ride.

"You're riding, I'm not."

"Huh?" The question hung in the air, his face blank. He finally turned to her and winked, but didn't answer.

Randall drove to the back of the ranch, where Rachel had not yet been. There was a large barn back there, with a riding ring nearby. He helped her out of the ATV and led her to a stall in the back of the barn. The cowboy named Tyler stood waiting for them.

"Rachel, meet Royal Blessing. He's our newest acquisition. And he's yours to ride."

Rachel stared at the Dutch Warmblood. The horse was exquisite, standing at least seventeen hands. His black coat gleamed under the lights. She held her hand out, palm up, and the horse nuzzled her fingers, taking in her scent. She moved her hand to his nose, and he tossed his head in greeting before nuzzling her hand again. Randall pulled a carrot out of his pocket and handed it to her.

"He's beautiful. But he isn't made for riding Western. He's from European stock and meant for riding English." And expensive, depending on his pedigree. She shoved that thought aside.

"That's why I bought him. You told me you used to ride in dressage events. I thought you would like the chance to ride again. And I plan to breed him. Start a new line of business here at the ranch."

"Actually, I do show jumping. But most show horses are gelded because stallions are too flighty and harder to train. Yours is not." Rachel kept her eyes on the horse as she spoke, admiring the intelligence in his eyes.

"No, Royal is not gelded. He is all male." Randall turned an intense look toward her.

"Wait a minute. Royal Blessing. I've heard that name. He's descended from a long line of Royals and is a Grand Prix winner."

"I knew you would probably recognize him." He turned back to Tyler. "How about if you go ahead and get Royal saddled for Rachel." Looking at Rachel he said, "We probably need to get you some new riding clothes and boots, too. Those will work for today, but you will want the full get up."

"Get up?" Rachel didn't understand.

"Outfit. Clothes. Get up."

Rachel laughed and shook her head. She had never heard such a ridiculous way to describe her clothes. Royal tossed his head in agreement. "I can get my own 'get up,' as you call it. It will give Annie and me another excuse to go shopping."

Fifteen minutes later, Rachel was astride the most magnificent horse she had ever seen, as they cantered around the large pen that Randall had set up behind the stable. She felt like she was floating as they made their way over a small course that had also been built. The jumps were short, but a good way to break in the skills that she had not used in a long time. Her heart beat in rhythm to his gait, her legs posting in the English riding style as her muscles remembered the moves. She would be sore tomorrow, but it would be a good sore.

She smiled at Randall who stood outside the pen, leaning on the rails of the fence. He had a gleam in his eye that she couldn't quite place. He seemed pleased, and she didn't know if it was with her or the horse. She focused on the next jump, horse and rider sailing smoothly over it together. She loved being back in the saddle, but she honestly couldn't say she loved this style any better than riding Astro free and uninhibited across the ranch. Kind of like her heart. She had kept it penned up and disciplined for so long. Could she be just as open with her heart to the man that was waiting for her just outside this pen?

After riding for a half hour, Rachel dismounted and handed the reins to Randall. "I love him! He's incredible! You made a very good purchase." Her blue eyes danced as she described the feeling of riding the horse.

"I'm glad you like him. I'm thinking of a mare to breed with him. Would you like to go along if I decide to go look her over? I could use your experienced input."

"I would absolutely love to go with you, Randall. Just let me know when."

"Will do. And in the meantime, Royal is yours to ride. Just come get me or Matthew before you do, please. If we can't be here, we can arrange for Tyler or one of the other ranch hands to assist."

Rachel sighed in pleasure. "Of course." It was a great surprise, she had to admit. But she hoped he hadn't done this solely for her.

Although she was living in a cabin at the ranch and they spent a lot of time together, they had made no commitments to each other as a couple. There had been no declarations of love from either of them. Still, every time he reached for her hand, she had a bit of a chill up her arm. And his kisses were wonderful—each one leaving a slow burn in her belly, filled with promise. He was a true Texas gentleman, treating her like a revered lady.

They made their way back to the cabin, where Annie came bouncing out the door to greet them.

"I found a condo, Mom. I made an offer on it yesterday, and it was accepted today. The seller has already moved out, so we can close in two weeks. I'm so excited!"

"That's great! A lot has happened in a short amount of time. And I know you want your own space." Rachel grinned. Her life had definitely taken a sharp turn the past few months, but she could see nothing but good things ahead.

FIFTEEN

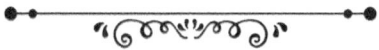

ANNIE DROPPED a brochure on the dining table. She had just come back to the cabin from closing on the condo. Furniture would be delivered over the next couple of days.

"What's this?" Rachel was puzzled.

"Read it." Annie sat back and waited, arms crossed.

"This is from the company that bought my house. Hudson Vacation Rentals. Where did you get it?"

Annie waved her hand. "Read the back, at the bottom. Fine print."

"A subsidiary of Hudson Holdings, Inc. Nora Hills, Texas. What is this, Annie? What does this mean?"

I found this at the title company. They said they do a lot of business with VacaRentals. They said Randall Hudson is mega-rich and owns several companies, which is why he has the holding company. The bottom line is, VacaRentals bought your house. VacaRentals is Hudson Holdings, and Hudson Holdings is Randall Hudson. Randall bought your house."

Rachel stared at the brochure. She hadn't made the connection when she sold the house.

"I saw something about Hudson Holdings in the title work at closing, but I just assumed it was named after the Hudson River. In New York. I didn't even question it." She wrinkled her brows together in thought. Did Randall do this? If so, she had been cheated once again.

"Mom. Are you okay?"

"He lied to me." Rachel put her hand over her mouth and swallowed the gall that threatened to spew as she whispered the words.

"Yup."

"We put the house up for sale to find out if this was God's will for our next steps. And he encouraged it. No, wait. I think it was his idea."

"Yes," Annie said. "He swooped in like a vulture."

"And I'm the road kill." Rachel sighed. "Like an armadillo on the side of the road. No match for his power and money."

"What are you going to do?"

"I need to leave. Looks like you still have a roommate. Is that okay?"

Annie headed toward Rachel's bedroom. "I'll help you pack."

RANDALL CLIMBED the steps to Rachel's cabin, whistling as he did. Smiling, he was looking forward to spending another Saturday with her. Watching her ride Royal gave him great pleasure, and he was amazed at her talent. He would have to build a bigger jump course, so that she could ride a more traditional pattern.

The door opened just as he lifted his hand to knock. "Randall."

"Good morning, Rachel. Are you ready to go?" She looked strained. He wondered if she was feeling well. She had cancelled on him last night without explanation.

"Come in, Randall. Have a seat at the table for a minute."

"Okay." Something was up. Randall looked around the cabin and found boxes, but he knew Annie was moving. He took off his hat and scratched his forehead as he sat down at the dining table, which held a folder from the title company.

Rachel looked up at the ceiling, blowing out a breath before looking around the room. Her arms were crossed, the fingers of one hand drumming across the opposite arm. Anytime Kate had acted like this, he knew she was about to give him the riot act about something. Rachel finally settled her gaze on him and leaned over the table, her hands flat on its surface.

"Do you own VacaRentals?"

Randall squinted his eyes, wondering where this discussion was going. "No, not exactly."

She placed the brochure on the table in front of him, the back of it facing up. "Annie found this at the title company yesterday when she closed on the condo. Read the fine print at the bottom."

Rachel was obviously upset, but he still didn't know why. "What am I looking for when I read this?" Rather than assume what was wrong, he wanted her to tell him.

"Hudson Holdings owns VacaRentals, and you own Hudson Holdings. Right?" Rachel stared him down, daring him to deny her accusation.

"Yes, that is technically correct." Randall furrowed his eyebrows together. "But I have several investors, too. Why is that a concern?"

"VacaRentals bought my house back in New York. Did you tell them to do that?" Now Rachel was pacing back and forth. Randall still wasn't sure what was wrong.

"I may have mentioned your house to the General Manager of the New York office."

"So when I said I would list the house to see if this was God's direction," she waved her hand through the cabin, indicating her move, "you swooped in and bought it."

"It wasn't quite like that." Randall looked down at the table, his hand flipping over the brochure.

"You manipulated me."

"What?" He looked up sharply at Rachel. Her gaze was angry, her eyes fierce. "No. I was just trying to help."

"But you failed to tell me what you were doing. Why didn't you just ask to buy the house? Why did you have to do something so underhanded?" Tears gathered in Rachel's eyes.

Randall still didn't understand why this was a problem, but he was starting to see that Rachel didn't like how it had all played out.

"You conned me. You lied to me. You cheated. You are no better than my husband—that lying snake."

"I did not cheat you. You got more than fair market value for that house. Is that what you are upset about?"

"So you *were* involved with the sale. Otherwise, how would you have known the final selling price? A million dollars? Really? Was it really worth that much, or were you just throwing your money around to get what you wanted?"

"Prices had skyrocketed since you originally bought the house. It was a seller's market. And you did get another offer, which was also very good. You could have taken that one." Randall didn't know what else to say. He didn't like the look on her face.

She sighed as a tear finally slipped down her face. "I think you need to leave. And I'm moving out."

"Rachel. Let's just go riding. We'll work this out." He stood, but didn't move away from the table.

"Go. Now. Please." She walked back to the front door and held it open, her meaning clear.

Randall placed his hat on his head and walked to the door, stopping as he came face to face with her. Pleading with his eyes because he knew by her body language that further words wouldn't work. She raised her eyebrows slightly and pointed out the door. Randall left in silence.

• •————————————• •

"HEY, Daddy. Where's Rachel? I thought she was going to ride Royal today." Matthew walked through the kitchen where Randall was sitting and poured himself a cup of coffee.

"She's not coming." Randall stared at his fingers, numb from his encounter with Rachel.

"Oh." Matthew sat the carafe back on the burner and pulled another cup from the cabinet. "Is something wrong?"

"I think I made a big mistake." Randall spoke so softly, Matthew puzzled his brow.

He poured another cup and handed it to his dad. "You mean with Rachel? Is she not what you thought she was?"

"She is everything I thought she was, and more. No, the mistake is mine."

"Tell me what happened." Matthew sat down at the table.

Randall explained about buying Rachel's house in New York, and her reaction to learning about it.

Matthew looked upward before focusing back on Randall. "I don't remember Mama ever getting bent out of shape over things like that."

Randall laughed, but it was bittersweet. "You have different memories than I do. Your mama could get riled up over the craziest things. Once, when we were first married, I bought her a really pretty bracelet for her birthday. Eighteen carat gold. She got mad. Said I should have spent the money on a new front door. That was before we remodeled the house. So for Christmas, I got her a new front door. You would have thought I got her a spider, the way she acted. I don't think I ever figured her out, but I sure had fun trying." Randall had his hand on his chin, his memories wistful.

"I didn't know about any of that."

"That was before you were born." Randall took a sip. His coffee was getting cold.

"Women get emotional about the strangest things. And you were just trying to help. I mean, she had just lost her job. What was she going to do if she stayed?" Matthew took a sip and winced at the bitter liquid. "I'm sure she will come around. Give her a few days. For now, let's focus on the guests coming in tomorrow."

Randall wasn't so sure.

SIXTEEN

RANDALL WAITED TWO WEEKS. Two long weeks. Rachel had left the ranch and moved in with Annie the same day as their rather passionate discussion. And he loved her passion. He loved the fury in her eyes that were the color of the Caribbean water stirred up after a storm. He just didn't like having that fury turned back on him.

He sent multiple text messages and called Rachel a couple of times, but she had not responded. He was not used to this. He was Randall Hudson, and he knew how to work a boardroom. Why couldn't he get a response from Rachel?

He picked up the phone and called his friend Jim over at Franklin Auto Mall. Jim had several stores with a wide variety of makes and models, and the Double H Ranch had a fleet contract with him.

"Jim Franklin," Jim answered his phone.

"Hey, Jim. This is Randall. Got a minute?" He sat down at the desk in his home office and leaned his elbows on the surface. He had been searching the Franklin Auto Mall website and found exactly what he was looking for.

"Anything for you, Randall. What's up?"

"I need a car. An Audi Q8, with all the bells and whistles. In blue. No, in teal-blue, to match the streak in her hair."

"Whose hair are we talking about, Randall? Have you been holding out on me?" Jim laughed.

"A lady I've been seeing. She was a guest at the ranch a few weeks ago, and now she has moved to Nora Hills. And I want to do something really nice for her. She needs a new car, and I want to surprise her." Randall was proud that he had come up with this idea. She was going to love it.

"You want to surprise her with a car? She must be one special lady. And you must be in love. Or in big trouble. Either way, I'm sure Kate would approve."

"She is special. I haven't even looked at another woman in the past three years. And she has a mind of her own, like Kate did. I can't wait to see her face when I surprise her."

Jim cleared his throat. "Randall, I seem to recall that Kate didn't like surprises. Are you sure your new woman will?"

"What woman doesn't want to be showered with nice things?" Randall twirled a pen between his fingers. Too bad he wouldn't be there to see her reaction.

"Alright, if you are sure. I don't have one in that color, but I can get it in a couple of days. Anything else you need?"

"I need it delivered directly to her. Here's her address." Randall gave Jim all of Rachel's information so that it could be licensed and titled in her name, and delivered straight to the condo. Now he would wait. If this didn't break the ice, he didn't think anything would.

RACHEL PEEKED out her window at her small front porch before answering her door. She was afraid that Randall would eventually show up in person, and she wasn't sure she would be able to throw him out again. But the man standing in front of her doorbell camera wasn't Randall. It looked like a delivery person.

"Can I help you?" Rachel opened the door a crack.

"Rachel Wilson?" The delivery man looked at her and the blue streak in her hair.

She opened the door wider. "Yes, I'm Rachel. What can I do for you?"

"I have a delivery for you. Sign here." The man handed his tablet toward Rachel. She pushed it back to him.

"I didn't order anything. What are you delivering?"

"I have a car from Franklin Auto Mall." The man pointed toward the parking lot where a teal-blue Audi Q8 was sitting.

"I didn't order a car. Who is it from?" Rachel had always wanted an Audi, but it was always beyond what she was able to spend.

"The order says it is from the Double H Ranch. They must like you over there." The man grinned.

Rachel furrowed her eyes at the car, then back at him. "The Double H sent it? Take it back. I don't want it."

"Excuse me?"

"I said take it back. I didn't order it, and I don't want it." Rachel crossed her arms.

"There is no cost to you, ma'am. It's already paid for." The young man wrinkled his brow and scratched his blond hair.

"Tell Randall Hudson he can. . . he can. . ." Rachel sputtered. How dare he? She glanced at her ten-year-old Toyota parked a few feet away. It's true, she could use a new car. Her battery died yesterday, and the mechanic suggested she would need a new timing belt soon due to its high mileage. That would be over a thousand dollars. Did Randall have his own personal grapevine checking up on her? But if so, what made him think he could just buy her a new car without even asking? *Is this supposed to be an apology for manipulating me, to get me to Texas? If so, he could take that car and shove it right down his* . . . She stopped her thoughts abruptly.

"Just take it back, please." Rachel sighed. Her beef with Randall wasn't any of this man's business. She closed the door with a firm click and marched into her kitchen, where the soup she made for lunch was getting cold. Now she would have to heat it up. Men. They were nothing but trouble.

●—————●

RANDALL'S PHONE RANG, and Jim Franklin's name popped up on the screen.

"Hey, Jim. How did it go? Did she like it?"

Jim chuckled, then stopped short. "Well, Randall, she declined delivery."

"She what? She mentioned once that she had always wanted an Audi. Did she want something else?"

"No, she said she didn't order it and didn't want it. And our delivery guy said he thought she was going to spit at him. Then she shut the door in his face. What did you do to her, Randall?"

Randall felt bluer than the streak in Rachel's hair. He was sure this would get him back into her good graces. "I messed up, Jim, that's what. I hurt her feelings, and I thought for sure the car would fix it."

"Man, that stinks. Women can be so fickle sometimes. I mean, who would turn down an Audi?"

"Yeah. Thanks anyway. You can take your normal fees, even though she sent it back."

"Good luck, man." Randall thanked him and hung up the phone. *What is wrong with women, anyway?*

<hr />

"WHAT CRAWLED up your britches and bit ya this morning?" Harris was the only one sitting at the round table. It was still early the next day, and the diner had just opened.

"Life." Randall held his cup up for the waitress to fill it.

"Life, or women?"

Harris was old enough to have been around the block several times. He probably knew everything there was to know about women. He was also rich enough to fund an entire team of psychiatrists for years. And none of the other guys were around. Randall lowered his voice.

"Rachel moved off the ranch to her daughter's condo."

"Why?" Years of wisdom filled a sea of wrinkles across Harris's face.

"She found out my company bought her house. She was furious."

"Hm. I hear there was also a horse and a car involved." The older man's eyes were sympathetic.

Randall raised his eyebrows. "Has the gossip mill already spread the story? Probably made up their own details, too."

"Well, this is the Table of Knowledge." Harris pointed to the sign over their heads.

Randall stirred his black coffee absently. "I thought I knew what women want, after thirty years of marriage. I mean, she's from New York. Don't city women like shiny, fancy things?"

"Randall, you will never learn everything there is to know about women." Harris smiled and raised an eyebrow. "My wife and I were married for nearly fifty years. She was telling me I was wrong, all the way up to the day she died. Best woman ever."

"She died a year ago, didn't she?"

"Yeah, and now she's dancing on angel's wings and worshipping her Savior." His gaze clouded with memories.

"Kate died three years ago. And I didn't realize I was lonely until I met Rachel. They're a lot alike. Both independent. When Kate would get her mind set on something, I couldn't stop her."

"And yet you are trying to stop Rachel." Harris looked over his reading glasses as the waitress set his breakfast in front of him.

"Stop her from doing what?" Randall scrunched his brows together.

"Whatever she wants to do. You're in love with her. That much is obvious. But does she love you?"

Randall shook his head. "It's too early for love, isn't it?"

"Is it?" The older man peppered his eggs. Almost black. How could he eat them that way?

Love. He hadn't even thought that word. He just knew he was miserable.

"So what is the answer?" Randall genuinely wanted to know.

Harris smiled as others from their round table group walked into the diner. "Son, every woman is different. If I tried to give you advice, you'd come back later and tell me it didn't work. So you're gonna have to figure this out for yourself. And I wish you luck. Cause if she's really as mad as you say she is, you might be waiting for a long time."

Randall threw some bills on the table to cover his coffee and Harris's breakfast, then stood and placed his hat on his head. He was not going to discuss his love life with the other guys. They were worse than a bunch of squawking chickens.

And he still didn't know what to do. But was he really in love with Rachel?

Randall drove to the back of the ranch and watched the Dutch Warmblood as he grazed in his special pasture. What was he doing? How had he become so smitten, so fast? He closed his eyes and basked in his memories. Everything about Kate that made him madly in love with her. Her perfume. Her love of horses. Her stubborn spirit. Her energy. Her resolve when things got tough. Their fights.

She bought the truck after one of their fights. It was his fiftieth birthday, and she wanted to go into San Antonio to celebrate. He had business calls that day and was tired afterward. The next day, she called Jim Franklin and bought the truck for him. He forgave her immediately.

The please-forgive-me gift worked for him. Why didn't the same thing work for Rachel? Looking around the truck, he realized he was hanging onto a memory. His memories. If it was time to move on, he needed to let them go.

SEVENTEEN

"WELCOME TO DEBBIE'S. Have a seat anywhere."

Rachel and Annie looked around the crowded diner. The smell of hot coffee and sweet syrup mingled with that of horses and leather.

Most of the tables were taken, but there was a small two-topper against a wall, near a large round table where several older men in overalls or Wranglers were sipping cups of coffee. Annie pointed to the smaller table, and they took their seats.

"Coffee?" The waitress held out the carafe.

"Yes, please. Room for cream." Rachel needed caffeine, and this was a different waitress than she had seen here before.

"We have the little individual cups. I'll be right back." One of the men from the round table called out as the waitress walked toward the back of the restaurant.

"Cheryl. Bring that pot over here, girl." The men all guffawed.

"Sweetums, you know where I'll pour this pot, right?"

Rachel watched the interaction, recalling the day she sat at their table, and they told her stories about Randall. The man swatted the waitress on her rear as she filled his cup, and she kissed him on the cheek. Must be another story there.

The menu had the normal diner fare. They looked around at other tables and saw a tantalizing array of eggs and bacon, pancakes, and waffles with fruit. Cheryl returned to their table and took their orders.

"Thanks for this, Annie. I needed it."

"Yeah, it's been a whirlwind couple of months, and I'm sorry I haven't been here more."

"That's okay. I wish you would let me help with the mortgage on the condo, though."

"No, Mom, that's your money. And I'm really sorry about everything that has happened. But I think maybe it was good to get out of New York, anyway. Despite the circumstances."

Rachel saw several heads turn at the table next door. They whispered and poked at each other, until the one closest to them stood up and ran his hand over his balding head. She thought some of the men looked familiar, but she didn't know this one.

"Excuse me, ma'am. We couldn't help but notice your hair. Are you Randall's lady?"

"Were you elected to ask?" Rachel raised one eyebrow. "I met some of your friends a couple of weeks ago."

Annie stood and stuck out her hand, intervening. "I'm Annie, and this is my mother, Rachel."

"I'm Ned, and this here is our breakfast group." He pointed over his head, where a piece of paper was stuck to a beam on the ceiling. They all stood slightly in greeting, and took their seats again.

"Table of Knowledge. Yes, I remember you. You told me a bit about Randall. But you failed to include some key points. Like he owns a giant corporation."

"Ah, heck, ma'am. He's not rich. At least, not as rich as me."

"He is, too. He runs that big corporation. Goes to Houston for meetings. Ain't never seen you in a suit, let alone in a board meeting." Earl knocked on the table.

"I am, too, rich. Just cause I don't spend it, don't mean anything. What I mean is, he's just one of us good ol' boys."

Ned was dressed in overalls and a worn flannel shirt.

The bald-headed man spoke up.

"I heard he was keeping company with a pretty lady from New York. I couldn't help but hear just now that you were from there. And, of course, your, um. . ." He waved his hand over his head to indicate her hair lock of blue.

Cheryl stopped at their table with their orders. Saved by the bell.

"It's nice to meet you all." Rachel picked up her fork. The waffles with strawberries and whipped cream looked heavenly.

"Same here, ma'am. And you, too, miss."

Ned sat down, but the smiles on the men's faces were more like those of little boys planning a bit of mischief. Maybe coming here this morning wasn't a good idea, after all.

Harris stood. "Gentlemen, let the ladies enjoy their breakfast." He walked around his table, past the men to Rachel, and held out his hand, which she took.

"Miss Rachel, I apologize once again. I hope our poor attempts at Texas hospitality won't send you running back to New York. We could use some fiery sophistication around here." He looked back at the round table and mouthed the words, "leave them alone," before exiting the restaurant.

Rachel smiled as Harris released her hand and left. It was good to see that someone still had manners, but the encounter left her wondering if he knew more than he had let on. She turned back to Annie, who took a bite of her breakfast.

"Tell me what happened about the car." Annie pushed her cleaned plate aside. Rachel lowered her head and spoke softly.

"I don't think this is the time or place." She nodded toward the circle of men, who had not moved since she and Annie had sat down at their small table.

Annie lowered her voice. "It's okay. They aren't listening."

The men had moved on to a story about Ned and an alligator. *Didn't they tell that same story the last time she was here?* Rachel snapped back to Annie.

"You told me some of it over the phone that day. It was an Audi, right? I looked them up online. It's a really nice car. Why did you send it back?"

Rachel ducked her head. She didn't want to discuss it here, but Annie persisted.

"Don't you think it's time to hear him out? Let him explain about the house again? And the car? I think he really likes you, and these guys seem to think so, too." She nodded her head slightly toward the round table. "I hate to see you alone and hurting."

"Did you forget that Randall lied about buying my house? I don't want a repeat of your father."

"Randall did not buy your house, Mom. Yes, his company did. But you also had other offers." Annie lifted her hand to stop Rachel's rebuttal, her voice a low but firm whisper. "Randall is not Dad."

Rachel huffed. "Annie, I have been on my own, raising you, paying the bills, making a life for us for the past fifteen years. I don't need another man coming along and trying to fix my life for me." The guys at the table glanced their way and she lowered her voice again. "I was doing just fine, thank you. There was nothing to fix." Except that she lost her job. She ignored that fact.

"Well, from what I gather from Matthew, guys down here in Texas think it is their duty to take care of their women. Don't you want somebody to pamper you? You don't want to be alone the rest of your life, do you?"

"You've been talking to Matthew? About us?"

Annie sat back in her chair. "Matthew is a nice guy, Mom. And we don't always talk about you and his dad."

Rachel surveyed her daughter's blue eyes. Eyes just like her own. Was she missing something? When had her daughter started looking out for her? Annie deserved to have a life, too.

•••————————••

RACHEL BECAME WITHDRAWN as the weeks passed. She made enough money from the sale of the house that she didn't have to work for at least a little while. She spent her days roaming around the condo, reading sappy romances that made her cry, watching sappy movies that made her cry even more, and eating too much chocolate. She stocked her freezer with instant meals delivered straight to her door so she didn't have to cook. She rose each morning, wandered through her day, most times without even changing out of her pajamas, and curled up in her bed at night. Annie tiptoed around her, giving Rachel the space that she said she wanted.

She felt bad that her daughter was caught in the middle of her mess. Annie would sometimes say she was "going out," and Rachel figured Annie needed separation from the drama. What she did while she was out, and who she was with, Annie didn't say. And Rachel didn't ask.

EIGHTEEN

RANDALL WATCHED through his window as Annie drove up to the ranch house Sunday afternoon. The sky was clear and sunny, the temperature hot, which was normal in July. Matthew stood on the front porch of the homestead as she pulled around the driveway, stopping in front of the house. Rachel found out Annie had met with him, she would be angry.

"Thanks for coming, Annie." Matthew walked down the porch steps and greeted her with a hug as she stepped out of her car. "Daddy is in the dining room. We have a small late lunch set out if you want to eat while we talk. I thought it might help relieve some of the stress."

Randall stepped away from the window as Annie followed Matthew through the house and into the dining room. She walked around the table and drew him into a full hug. "Hello, Mr. Hudson."

"It's Randall, Annie. You know that." He smiled slightly and let her hug him, the embrace giving him hope.

Pitchers of different beverages sat on an antique sideboard

along with a glass jar of ice water with a spout at the bottom. The water was infused with fruit, lemon and lime slices, and cherries. Matthew poured drinks for everyone and sat down at the table next to Annie. Randall sat at the head of the large table.

They chit-chatted for a bit, picking at finger foods before Randall finally asked, "How is Rachel?" He couldn't hide the sadness in his face. He knew he had done something terribly wrong, he just wasn't sure what that was.

"Mom looks a lot like you do." Randall nodded, appreciating Annie's direct answer.

"I don't know what to do, Annie. Matthew thinks you might be able to give me some insight, or at least another idea of how to reach out to her."

Annie sat up straight. "Let's talk about what happened first. You bought her house."

"I didn't buy her house. I really had nothing to do with it."

"But your company did, and you knew about it. Mom said that was not honest." He fidgeted when she fixed her eyes on him.

He lowered his face and focused on his glass of water, sliding it back and forth between his hands. Condensation dripped down the sides, and he swiped a trail in it with his finger.

"Then you bought her a horse. But not just any horse. A champion showjumper. A three-hundred-thousand-dollar horse. Some breed from Europe, according to Mom. And yeah, I looked up the sale online." She continued staring at him. He shifted his gaze away.

"Then you bought her a car. Without asking her. Even though what you bought was perfect for her, I might add." That made Randall look up from the glass. "Mom almost called the dealership back and told them she wanted it anyway. But you didn't hear that part from me." Annie held her hands together in front of her chin and pointed at Randall with her index finger, indicating she approved of the car, but not the gesture.

"So what did I do wrong? My daddy always said you should go big or stay at home. I never go halfway on a business decision." He tilted his head, perplexed.

"But this isn't business. Or poker." She looked him straight in the eye, pointing her finger on the table between them. "Randall, you can't buy a woman's affection. Well, maybe some women like that stuff, but you can't buy Mom's. Or mine either, for that matter." She placed her hand on his arm. "Mom wants to be appreciated. She wants you to be interested in what she wants, not just what you want, or what you think she would want."

"That's why I bought the horse. I know she used to ride in competitions, and even rode at the National Horse Show in her twenties." Randall looked at Matthew, who shrugged. "What was wrong with that?" He turned his hands up quizzically.

Annie leaned her head back before looking at Randall again. "You paid three hundred thousand dollars for a horse! Who does that?"

"He's a good horse. And I can breed him with the mare I'm buying. Their foals will be valuable too, and we'll have our investment back in no time. I thought Rachel would appreciate that."

"But you didn't ask her, first." She leaned across the table. "You just did it. Then told her it was hers."

"Hers to ride."

"Is there a difference?" Annie raised an eyebrow. "No one else around here even knows how to ride English."

Randall sat silent for a few minutes. They picked further at the food, none of them really interested in eating, but needing something to do in the silence. He looked at Matthew, who returned the gaze with an I-have-no-clue look on his face.

"What do I do now?" He resigned himself to his fate.

"Start with flowers. But don't buy her roses."

"Why not?" Randall was confused. He thought every woman liked roses.

"Because Dad always bought roses for Mom after cheating on her."

Ouch. "Okay. No roses. So what do I get?"

At this point, Matthew spoke up. "How about talking to Jenny down at the flower shop? I have seen some of her arrangements, and they are great. She might have ideas about what kind of flowers to send."

⋅———⋅

RANDALL WALKED into the flower shop Monday morning and bumped into a bell that rang over his head as he entered. It was one of those antiques that tinkled when the door opened and closed. The sound brought Jenny from the back of the store.

"Randall! Hey, I haven't seen you in a while. What can I do for you? Need a big bouquet for that lovely woman of yours?" Did the entire town know about Randall's infatuation with Rachel?

"Yes, but actually, I would like some ideas from you first. I kind of have to apologize to her."

"Oh. Red roses it is. And lots of them. Another customer came in last week and got three dozen. It must have been a doozy of a fight." She pulled out her book of arrangements for Randall to browse.

"No, I'm afraid roses won't do. It needs to be unique, and

send a message." He explained the situation to Jenny, who raised her eyebrows high, eyes wide as he told the story.

"Wow. If a man did that for me, I would be thrilled. Then I would conk him over the head with my iron skillet. What in the world were you thinking?"

Randall sighed. "Apparently, I wasn't. Or at least, that's what I have been told." He flipped the pages in the book. Everything he saw was typical and didn't really convey what he thought he needed to say. There were roses, which he had already dismissed, along with arrangements for birthday, sympathy, and congratulations. He started to give up when he saw an arrangement that said 'discontinued' across the page. "What's this?" The flower arrangement stared back at him, googly eyes and all. "Why is this discontinued? Can you do something like this?" He pointed at the flower.

"You know, that might be just the thing." Jenny wrote down the number on the page. "The big mum has been discontinued by my normal supplier, but I might be able to find it somewhere else. Give me the afternoon to check. What would you like to say on your card?"

They sat down at a table, pouring over the arrangement and the message Randall thought he needed to send. Jenny added a few of her own to Randall's list, based on how she knew a woman would feel under the circumstances. Randall was going to have to eat crow, that was for sure. They plotted together, working out their strategy. When Randall left the shop, he felt a little more hopeful.

NINETEEN

RACHEL WALKED through the condo as the doorbell rang a second time. "I'm coming! And you better not be Randall!" It wouldn't surprise her to find him standing there.

She opened the door to see a young man holding a flower arrangement. "Delivery for Mrs. Wilson."

Rachel took the flowers from the young man. "Let me get you something for a tip."

"I don't need a tip, ma'am. It's been covered." He grinned under his ball cap.

"Okay, then. Thank you." She closed the door and walked to the dining table just as Annie entered from her bedroom.

"What's that, Mom?" Rachel removed the tissue covering the flowers, expecting to see roses. Instead, she found a giant yellow mum surrounded by greenery and baby's breath. But the flower had two large googly eyes—the kind found in craft stores—glued to it to make a face. A black pipe cleaner had been bent into a frown, and another one was wound into a tight ball to make a nose.

More pipe cleaners had been cleverly bent to create a body,

arms, and legs for the flower. A toy cowboy hat sat on top of the flower, and little toy boots covered the feet. The two hands were holding a card in front of the flower with a simple message on it.

"I'm sorry. – Randall"

Rachel and Annie looked at each other and laughed at the same time.

"That's it?" Annie looked through the tissue for another card. "That's pretty lame, even if he is cute."

"Yeah, he's going to have to work a lot harder than this to impress me." Rachel picked up the vase and walked toward the trash can, prepared to throw it all away, even while she smiled inwardly.

"Don't do that, Mom! You have to admit, at least he tried. And the arrangement is unique. Let's leave it on the table for a few days. Just to brighten up the place, if nothing else." Annie snapped a picture with her phone.

"What are you doing?" Rachel frowned.

"Just taking a pic to remember this by. I might have a man want to apologize to me someday, and I want to tell him what not to do."

"Well, it won't work, that's for sure." Rachel shook her head and walked into the kitchen. She could still see the flower from there, staring at her as if it was pleading Randall's case. She wasn't going to have that thing looking at her all night long. She picked it up and moved it to a corner table in the living room, where it was not readily seen. The cowboy hat drooped when she moved it. She looked at it again, then turned back to the kitchen. She would not budge. She Would Not.

Rachel's doorbell rang the next morning while she was in the shower. Annie sat at the dining room table, laptop in front of her, working on a marketing plan for one of her customers.

"Flowers for Mrs. Wilson." He grinned widely when he saw Annie instead of Rachel.

"Wow. You're pretty. Maybe someday I will bring flowers for you."

Annie thanked the young man for the flowers and the compliment. Closing the door, she walked to the dining room and set the flowers on the table.

"What's that? More flowers?" Rachel dropped the towel from her head as she walked into the room, shaking out her curls as she walked. She had just freshened the blue streak in her hair, needing to make it brighter. It was, after all, her reminder not to be taken in by a smooth-talking man.

"You do the honors, Mom. What do you think he sent this time?" There was no doubt the flowers were from Randall.

Rachel peeled back the tissue to reveal another mum, only this one was pink. It was similar to the first, but the eyes had lids that were halfway down, and the mouth was in a more exaggerated frown. The hands were clasped together and held another card.

"I was wrong. Please forgive me. – Randall"

Rachel put her hands to her face. She wasn't ready to forgive him. Not yet. She knew that Jesus said if she had anything against her brother, she should go to him. But she had too many memories of too many "let's try agains" with her ex. She had to stick to the promise she had made to herself fifteen years ago.

"What are you going to do, Mom?" Annie said the words softly, taking another picture.

Rachel picked up the vase and set the arrangement with the other one on the corner table. "I'm not going to do anything." She turned away and walked back into the bedroom, shutting the door with a determined click.

The next two days were similar to the first. More mums

were delivered, each in a pose that reflected the message on the card.

"I miss you."

"How do I fix this?"

She removed the tissue on that one carefully, revealing the flower, which held a toy wrench in one hand and a hammer in the other. It had a small toy toolbelt around the skinny waist. But the thing that made Rachel sit down to stare at it was the tear that dripped from one eye, and she thought of the verse from Psalms about how God collects her tears and puts them in a bottle.

She stood and walked into the living room. Then she carefully picked up each flower and moved them from the corner table onto the dining room table, creating a small group of cowboys. All they needed were their horses. Rummaging through Annie's closet, she found the collectible horses that she had given Annie over the years, amazed that her daughter still kept them. Tenderly carrying them in her arms, she placed one beside each cowboy mum. Then she laid her head on the table and cried.

Randall was breaking through. Rachel felt the warmth of her daughter's hand on her shoulder for just a moment. Then Annie went to her room, picked up the remaining three horses in what she called her 'herd,' and placed them on the table with the others. Rachel heard the camera click, but ignored the tug at her heart.

Flowers continued to come daily. "I've fallen for you." made Rachel chuckle. The flower was lying down, hands and booted legs in the air, hat behind the flower as if it had come off during the fall.

"I'm head over heels for you."

This flower was standing on its head, hands on the ground on either side of the mum, and booted legs up in the air.

"You've lassoed my heart." This one made Rachel laugh outright. The flower held a tiny toy lasso, a stuffed red heart in the center. Rachel had begun placing the most recent flower on the kitchen island, in a place of prominence.

"I'm yours forever."

The mum stared off into the distance, stars twinkling overhead in a display of eternity. Annie took a picture of each flower as it was received.

"Annie, have you been spying on me? Are you sending pictures of these flowers to Randall?" Rachel was peeling potatoes with a plaintive look on her face.

"No, Mom. I'm not sending anything to Randall. But Matthew and I have been talking." Annie picked up another knife and started peeling alongside Rachel. "We don't like seeing the two of you so sad."

"Randall's been sad?" She hadn't considered that. She just thought he was trying to manipulate her, as if it was another game.

Maybe I've misinterpreted things. She reverently placed the mum with the others.

TWENTY

"HEY, MAN. WHERE YOU BEEN?"

Randall pulled a chair away from the round table and sat down with his friends, who all looked at him curiously.

"Been busy. Ranch business, board meetings. You know. The usual."

"Do you usually send flowers to a pretty lady? We saw her here a couple of weeks ago. She's quite a looker. All the way from New York City."

"Ned, I hope you didn't say anything stupid." Randall picked up a tiny tub of cream and tossed it at his friend.

Earl guffawed. "No more than usual. Asked her if she was your lady. She said she was nobody's lady."

"She can be my lady if you don't want her."

Randall glared at Ned, even though he knew the man was just teasing. They would never step in on each other's women. A waitress he didn't know sat a plate of biscuits and gravy in front of him. Where was Cheryl?

"But what's up with those flowers? Sending them every

day? You're making us all look bad, man." Mike was one of the new guys at the table.

"Where did you hear that?" Gravy dripped to his plate as Randall held his fork in the air.

"Harris has been courtin' Jenny."

Randall gave them his best you've-gotta-be-kidding-me look. Harris was old enough to be Jenny's father. They all ate in silence for a few minutes until one of them cleared his throat.

"Is it true? And is it working? I might need some advice on how to apologize." The new guy had just married his third wife.

"What did you do, Mike?"

"I didn't do nuthin.' Well, okay, I might have grinned at a pretty lady while we were walking around the square."

"Oh, was that all? She'll forgive that. Maybe you should buy her a new car." Ned chuckled at his joke.

"If all you guys can do is give me a hard time, I'd be better off talking to Rocket. At least he doesn't talk back." Randall took the last bite of his breakfast.

"Ha. Maybe you should have talked to him first. He might have the best advice." They all laughed and elbowed each other.

Randall drained his cup. "Thanks for the laughs, guys. Mike, you take care of your new wife. There might not be another one willing to put up with you."

Randall felt the eyes on his back as he left the diner. What was he going to do if Rachel wouldn't forgive him?

•——————•

THE CLOCK on the stove told Rachel she had not even slept four hours. Insomnia had been her companion lately, and she thought that staying up until almost midnight would make her tired enough to sleep through the night. It didn't work.

Her grandmother had always told her this was the time of night when lost souls roamed the earth looking for peace. While she didn't believe that old wives' tale, she had to admit that her soul was disturbed. Dreams of Randall, the subtle thud of his boots, his wide smile, A-list jaw, and sexy mix of leather, horse, and sunshine kept her tossing and turning. Giving in to the inevitable, she paced the floor before finally stopping at her balcony doors.

"Okay, God. You got me up in the middle of the night. What are you trying to tell me?"

There was no answer.

"Am I supposed to just ignore what he did?"

The dark condo was quiet inside, while outside the occasional noisy car drove by. Dogs barked at each other. Two cats raced across the parking lot, one chasing the other. A garbage truck pulled into her complex to pick up the overflowing dumpster, dropping it with a thud that was loud enough to wake the neighborhood.

"What am I doing here, anyway, God? Why am I in Texas? Why did you bring us here? Why did you bring *me* here? Was that really you speaking when Randall bought my house?"

The silence continued.

The moon hovered over the parking lot, yawning before its descent behind the horizon. Lights came on across the street as someone woke up to begin another day.

The diner would open in a couple of hours. The owners were probably already there, preparing the made-from-scratch buttermilk biscuits and gravy that was a staple item on their menu, and cutting up strawberries for the waffles and whipped cream that was also popular. She could almost smell the delicious concoctions from here. But she would stay away from the breakfast crowd. She didn't need Randall's friends from the Table of Knowledge giving her more advice. Who decided that the men had all the knowledge, anyway?

She turned from the sliding glass door and walked to the dining table that was full of flowers. She leaned down to sniff the one delivered yesterday, careful of the goofy face. Giant mums, each with a different message, begged her to forgive Randall for his deceptions. He hadn't really lied, per se, like her husband did. And he hadn't committed fraud, like her company executives did. But he had taken over her life, swooping in like a knight in shining armor, riding in on a white horse to save the damsel in distress. Or a cowboy riding in to save the day, ready to lasso the hombre trying to tie her to the train tracks. Only thing was, she wasn't a damsel in need. Well, maybe a little need. But she didn't like his method for saving her.

Annie said that Randall was sad. The mere fact that Annie knew that tidbit felt like another betrayal, this time by her daughter. Was she wrong to hold out? What was she holding out for? And what would it take to satisfy the emptiness that was keeping her awake at night?

The next day the doorbell rang again. Rachel opened it, expecting to see the same young man that had been delivering the flowers and winking at Annie each time. She thought he might have a crush on her daughter. But it wasn't him. It was an older woman.

"Mrs. Wilson? I'm Jenny. I own the flower shop. Can I come in, please?"

Rachel stepped back and motioned for Jenny to come in. They went to the dining room table, which by this point was nearly filled with flowers. The first one was starting to fade, its petals falling to the table.

"Is this your handiwork?" Rachel indicated the flowers as

she set the last delivery down. "I must say, you've been pretty clever."

"Do you have a few minutes to talk? Woman to woman, please?"

"Sure, do you want some coffee?"

"Coffee would be wonderful."

For the next hour, the women commiserated. Jenny was candid, telling the story of how Randall had come to her, completely heartbroken and not knowing what to do to win Rachel back. Rachel explained her position, but began to understand what Randall was doing. Jenny had created the flowers, but the messages came from him.

Jenny looked at her, taking her hand to get her full attention. "Rachel, that man loves you. I can keep sending flower arrangements every day. He says he will send them as long as it takes. But I have to tell you, you are breaking his heart." She nodded at today's delivery, still covered in tissue. "Go ahead and open this one."

The mum was yellow, with the same cowboy hat and boots. One hand held the lasso, but it was drooped to the side, hands down in defeat. A small red heart was attached to the body, a split down the middle of the heart. Tears fell from each eye.

A horse had been added to the display. It looked like the Dutch Warmblood that Randall had purchased for her. A tiny crystal tear clung to the horse's face.

Rachel placed her hand over her mouth and closed her eyes, trying to stop her own tears that threatened to spill over her cheeks. Opening them again, she smiled grimly at Jenny. Taking a deep breath, she searched for the card, which she found propped in the greenery.

"Please say something."

That was all it took. Tears now flowed freely. Her heart had been stirred, like a tidal pool threatening to engulf her. Jenny reached forward to hug Rachel, and the two embraced, both of them sobbing. It was the release that Rachel needed.

"What do I do?" Rachel sniffed and moved back to her chair. Reaching for a box of tissues on the counter, she placed the box between them, taking a tissue for her nose, which was turning red. "Can I send a flower back to him?"

"It would be my honor. In fact, this one is on the house." Jenny smiled, wiping her own tears. "What would you like it to say?"

•————•

RANDALL LOOKED up from the website he was reading as Matthew entered the family room. Matthew held a bundle in his hands, the item wrapped in tissue paper.

"Daddy, I have a delivery for you." He paused before continuing. "Jenny brought it."

"Is it from Rachel?" Randall didn't want to hope too much.

"Why don't you open it and see?" Matthew set the arrangement down on the coffee table that was in front of the sofa.

Randall sat up, blinking his eyes that had become blurry from looking at cattle prices. He stared at the large delivery for several minutes, afraid to find out what was inside. Finally, he lifted his hand and removed a small piece of tissue. Stopping, he peeked inside to see a mum. He continued removing the tissue, wondering if the message would be positive, or if she was gone forever.

The mum was yellow, which gave him hope. He was afraid it would be dyed black, or red in anger. He removed the rest of the paper to find a second mum. Each flower held a toy cell phone.

The first mum had a blue streak in its hair, and the second

mum had the same cowboy hat and boots that were on the flowers he sent to Rachel. Randall looked up at Matthew. "What do you think this means?"

"Well, this fell out as I was bringing it inside the house." Matthew handed him a card.

"Call me."

Randall whooped and reached for his phone.

TWENTY-ONE

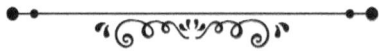

RACHEL HEARD the knock on the door and hurried to straighten the blue top she had paired with her gray slacks. Calming herself, she opened the door to find Randall standing there with a bouquet of colorful zinnias in his hand and a sheepish grin on his face. He also held a take-out bag from Wing and a Prayer BBQ. He looked half sorry and half excited. She backed away from the door and swept her hand for Randall to come in.

He walked through the door, confident swagger missing from his stride. Clean-shaven, hair neatly combed, and a white chambray shirt today, starched and pressed. His favorite bolo hugged his collar, looking like it might be choking him.

"Hi, Randall."

"Hey, Rachel. I brought dinner." He held up the bag.

Rachel took the flowers to the kitchen and found a vase. She had somewhat of a collection, having received so many flowers from him over the past two weeks. Some were still fresh, and she had them displayed on her dining room table.

"Bring the food this way and set it on the table. I'll get some plates and silverware."

"Rachel." He had taken off his hat and was flipping it over and over in his hands.

She took the hat from him and held up her hand. "Let's save the heavy stuff for later and focus on dinner."

"Okay. Where is Annie tonight?"

"Annie got all dressed up and went out. I think she wanted to give us space."

"That's interesting. Matthew also got all dressed up and went out. Do you suppose they are together?"

Rachel set plates, forks, and napkins on the table. "That's possible. She did say they were talking. Would that be weird, them being together?"

"Why?"

"I don't know. Us, and our kids. It just seems strange."

"They aren't kids anymore, Rachel." He pulled a box of barbeque out of the sack.

"Yeah, I know. Maybe that's why it's strange."

They finished their dinner and cleaned up the take-out boxes and the dishes. Randall took one of Rachel's hands in his. "Can we talk now?"

"Let's go out on the balcony." She led him to the sliding doors just off the living area, and pulled him to a gliding davenport.

"Rachel, I need to apologize." They had barely sat down.

"Okay. I appreciate that. But what are you apologizing for?" She wanted to mend things, but wasn't going to make it easy for him. Her ex was great at issuing random apologies that he didn't mean.

"Annie came over the other day and set me straight. I think I need to explain some things."

"Go on."

Randall cleared his throat and rubbed his hands along his thighs. He was clearly nervous.

"Life in New York is a lot different than life here in Texas. Expectations are different. Annie reminded me that you have been independent for a few years. You have done everything for yourself, and even raised her during the last of her teen years and put her through college."

"That's right. So how is that different from anywhere else?"

"In Texas, men are raised to take care of their women."

Rachel quirked an eyebrow at him.

"Oh, we know that women are strong. Don't get me wrong. I mean, Kate was a lot like you. Strong, independent, and sometimes scary." He chuckled, then cleared his throat. "In New York, it may seem like we are trying to be controlling. But in Texas, we cherish our women." He hoped that would be enough.

"Randall, I have been taking care of myself, and Annie, and project teams installing software in large companies throughout the country, for the last fifteen years. I do not need a man to take care of me."

"But I need you. I want you. And I want to cherish you." Randall repeated the statement, fiddling with his hands as he pleaded with her.

"You see this streak of blue?" She flipped her hair with her fingers. "I put it there after my divorce. To remind me that I will never allow a man, or anyone, to control me, manipulate me, con me, or manage my life for me ever again."

She pointed to her Bible, lying nearby on a side table. She had been reading it just this morning to prepare herself for today's talk with Randall. *"I can do all things through Christ, who strengthens me."* She made air quotes when she said "through Christ."

"And what about the man's role in the family? Isn't that

ordained by God?" He picked up the Bible and flipped it open to Ephesians, quickly picking out the verse he was referring to. "Wives, submit yourselves to your husbands."

Rachel shook her head. If this was his attitude, they were done. She took a cleansing breath. "First of all, I'm not your wife." Yet. She couldn't stop the thought. "Secondly, keep reading." She pointed further down the page.

Randall read where Rachel was pointing. *"Husbands, love your wives, just as Christ loved the church and gave himself up for her."*

"Exactly. *Gave himself up for her.* You directed a company that you own to buy my house. Without my knowledge." Rachel took another breath and held up one finger. She wasn't done. She held up a second finger.

"You paid three hundred thousand dollars for a horse, without my knowledge, that you wouldn't have bought otherwise, just so I can ride English instead of Western." She huffed a breath. "Then you bought a car—a ninety-thousand-dollar car—and had it delivered to me. Once again, without asking me." She held up three fingers and pointed them at him. "How does that cherish me? You've spent over a million dollars on me without asking me first. Who does that kind of stuff, anyway?"

Randall hung his head. "Yeah, that's pretty much how Annie summed it up."

Rachel paused, lowering her voice. "Whose idea were the mums? Those were nice."

"Annie's. She told me not to send roses because her dad used to do that every time he did something wrong. Only she didn't quite use those words."

"Annie has strong feelings about her father. I wish she had better memories." Rachel lamented the many times she had tried to work things out with her ex. Sometimes she regretted ever meeting him. But then she wouldn't have Annie. Still, she knew that their daughter had been hurt badly, too.

"Randall, I don't need flashy things. I know that you have enough money to do those kinds of things for me, and maybe Katherine appreciated them. But I don't want to just hang on somebody's arm and let him do all my thinking for me. I want..." Rachel stopped. She thought she was happy being single, but she was feeling more lonely every day.

"So where do we go from here?" Randall fidgeted with his thumbs. "My daddy and granddaddy had both taught me to be the caretaker of the family. I taught Matthew to do the same, and hope that someday Matthew will have a family of his own to care for.

Rachel considered his question. Should they go anywhere from here? She had to admit that she really did like him. She was strongly attracted to him. She could even see a future with him. But right now?

"I need someone who is constant. Stable." She took his hand and linked their fingers together, resting them on his knee. "Let's just be us for a while, okay? Hang out together and do things together. But you have to stop making decisions for me."

He bumped the tip of his boot on the concrete deck, the glider moving back and forth as he shifted. "That sounds like being friends. I was hoping for more." He looked up at her, a bit like a puppy dog wanting a pat on the head.

Rachel blew a breath, causing that beautiful blue streak to flutter. "I think any strong relationship has to be built on friendship. Don't you? If we can't be friends, how can we ever be anything more? We rushed our relationship so quickly, we blew right past being friends."

Randall nodded, his face pensive.

"But we can be really close friends." Had she said that out loud?

Randall grinned.

"And one more thing. I do need a new car. You were right about that. Do you think Jim still has that teal-blue Audi?"

Randall grinned and pulled out his phone. "Let's find out."

She put her hand out to stop him. "But, Randall, I'm buying the car—not you. I made plenty of money from the sale of my house. I can afford it, and I want to do it myself. It was your money that bought it, anyway. Understand?"

Randall put his arm around Rachel, squeezing her shoulders. "Sure thing. What time should I pick you up in the morning?"

"We'll have to take my car, since I want to trade it in. Is nine o'clock too early?"

"Honey, I'm a rancher. I'm up and at 'em by five. I'll be here at nine." He clicked on Jim's name in his contact list and sent a quick text. "Now, what about making up?"

She moved closer and placed her forehead on his. "Well, you know, I was just thinking. . ."

That was all the acknowledgement he needed. Cupping his hand on the side of her face, he placed a slow, lingering kiss on her lips. She returned every action with one of her own.

And somewhere in the back of his mind, he decided to sell his truck.

TWENTY-TWO

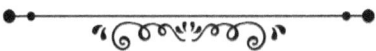

RACHEL READIED herself for the next jump. Hands steady on the reins, she clinched her knees just before they reached the bars, trusting the horse. Muscles gathered under her, the powerful animal was sure-footed and confident. Leaning forward, they sailed over the jump together, and she relaxed in the saddle as they continued to the next jump. Royal was loving the challenge, ears perked and eyes focused. He was magnificent, and she could see how he had won so many events.

The last time she had ridden like this, she was pregnant with Annie. It wasn't long before the riding had to stop. Then she and her husband moved to New York for his job, and riding was no longer important. Instead, she fought for her marriage for the next five years, before finally losing her husband to another woman. Now she was back in the saddle, thanks to the man watching her traverse the course.

Her eyes flitted to him where he stood just outside the arena, one booted foot on the bottom rail. Randall watched as they rode together, tracking their every movement as his head followed them around the course. When she reached the end, she reined Royal over to the fence.

"What do you think?" Randall draped his arms over the top rail to rub Royal's nose.

"I think it is a shame he is retired. He could probably go another year or two." She shielded her eyes, missing the wide-brimmed Stetson she wore when she was on Astro. Randall had taken her shopping for the appropriate garments of buff-colored breeches, knee-high boots, a dark gray show coat, and a black velvet helmet. They were great for riding the jump course, but the helmet did little to block the bright Texas sun.

"That may be true, but we don't want to miss the window of opportunity for breeding. As it is right now, we have to keep him away from mares to keep him and the mare safe. That is why we have him stabled here on the backside of the ranch. We'll collect the sperm and inseminate."

Rachel turned her head to hide her burning cheeks. She was fully familiar with the process, but talking about it with Randall stirred things inside her that needed to stay quiet. Royal, on the other hand, shifted under her as if he knew his future was being discussed. She didn't know how much a colt sired by Royal would bring, but imagined it would be pricey for the buyer, and good income for the ranch.

"You also said you were looking for a mare. Does that mean you intend to start them for resale?"

"You think you could do that?"

"Without a doubt. It takes time, but yes. I could do it."

"Well, there's your answer then. Why don't you take Royal around the course again, now that he has had a breather."

Rachel nudged Royal's shoulder with her knee and turned him toward the first jump. Flying around the course on this exceptional horse was like floating through the air, her stomach rising and falling with each jump, her breaths free and light.

When they reached the water hazard, she held her breath, anticipating the splash as his hooves touched down. At the end of the course, Royal tucked his nose to his breast, knowing he had completed a perfect circuit. Rachel leaned forward to hug him around his neck before dismounting.

"So did I make a good purchase?" Randall walked across the arena to them.

"Yes, I have to admit it. Given his skill and pedigree, you probably got a good deal."

"I did it for you, Rachel. I want you to be happy."

Their eyes met, and he lifted one of her hands to his lips, lightly kissing her fingers. The action made her blush. She had not been treated like she mattered in a very long time. And now that she understood his motives, she decided to relax and let him pamper her. But she still didn't have a job. And she didn't want to get into another situation where she lost her identity to the man doing the pampering.

•+————————•

"RANDALL, I have to ask you something." Rachel hesitated, unsure about the next question, but needing to have an understanding of what kind of man Randall really was. It was a Friday afternoon, the sun was high in the sky, and they had ridden Rocket and Astro out to their favorite spot on the smaller lake in the back of the ranch.

She played with a corner of the blanket they were sitting on, her legs curled to one side. Randall was stretched out fully on his side, his arm curled over her legs as she sat. A breeze tugged at her hair.

"Shh. Sit still for a minute." Randall held up his finger to stop her question.

"What's wrong?"

"The birds have stopped. Look up into this tree. There are three birds up there, and they have all stopped, like they are frozen. One bird is even hanging upside down. Must be a woodpecker." His words were whispered, and he flicked his finger to point in the direction of the birds without scaring them.

"What does that mean? Why are they frozen?" Rachel squinted her face, her voice soft.

"Usually means there is a predator in the area." He glanced around them, then overhead. "There. There it is. High up in the tree. A huge hawk."

Rachel pointed her eyes up, trying to focus on the highest branches. There, in the very top, sat a red-tailed hawk. "So what does this mean?" She spoke quietly and asked again. The bird was exquisite.

"Folklore says it means an angel is passing by. Native Americans say it means something sacred is about to take place. Reality says danger is near. The birds will stay frozen until the hawk moves. May take several minutes. Hawks have been known to sit and watch for animals for hours."

They laid back on the blanket and watched the birds, which stayed completely still until the hawk finally flapped its wings and rose into the sky. The birds then resumed their activity, as if nothing had just happened. It made Rachel shudder when taken in context with what she was about to ask.

"Okay. You were saying?" Randall focused on Rachel. At least he was smiling.

"That was a pretty good segue into my question." She hoped that lightened the impact of what she was going to say. "You know I'm not a predator, right? I mean, you have to know by now I'm not after your money. I'm not like that hawk." She shifted as she asked the question, nervous about how he would answer.

He laughed and rolled onto his back, looking up at her with his warm brown eyes. "Yes, I think you have made that perfectly clear."

"Good." She relaxed—a little. "So please take this next question in that light." She cleared her throat. "Just how big is Hudson Holdings?" *That wasn't the same as asking 'How much money do you have?' Was it?*

"You mean you haven't Googled it?" He sat up, taking her hand.

"Annie probably has. But if so, she hasn't said anything to me."

"Well, if you did, you would find out that Hudson Holdings is a privately owned corporation that has several subsidiaries. I'm the CEO and President, Matthew is the CFO and COO. We own the bulk of the shares, but we also have some investors. And we are investors in other companies."

"What kind of subsidiaries?"

"Oh, you know. This is Texas. Oil, gas, stuff like that."

Oil? "That was a pretty vague answer."

He played with her hand. Maybe he was unsure of what she would think. "I wanted to give you a picture of how we are structured. You were a program manager. You know this stuff makes a difference. So to answer your question directly, altogether, we are in the eleven-digit range. The actual net worth varies from day to day. But it's about a seventy-thirty split with our investors, and a sixty-forty split between what Matthew and I own. I handed off quite a bit to Matthew after Katherine died."

"So buying my house was. . ."

"No hit to our budget at all, actually." She flopped back on the blanket at his words. He laid down beside her and kissed the top of her head, tucking her in close as he wrapped his arm around her. "Does that make a difference? To us? I'm still just me. And I'm going to love you anyway."

Rachel placed her arm over her eyes, trying to comprehend what she had just learned. A million dollars was pocket change to him. Yet as she looked around the ranch, she didn't see evidence that he liked to live the lifestyle of the rich and famous. He sat here today on a blanket with her, in his normal worn jeans, blue chambray shirt, and brown work boots. His hat, while it was a Stetson, was stained with years of sweat from working outside with cattle, fences, ditches, and anything else that needed attention. He worked just as hard as the cowboys that he housed in a nice dorm-type building on the other side of the large lake. And yet, he was also a corporate mover and shaker. She could imagine him at the head of the table in an executive conference room full of powerful men. He was probably a major donor to political campaigns, too.

And had he just told her that he loved her?

TWENTY-THREE

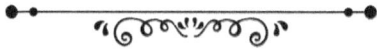

RACHEL'S PHONE rang and connected with the Bluetooth on her new car. She was stuck in traffic, on her way to the ranch, so she hit the button to connect without thinking. She didn't recognize the number on the caller ID.

"Hello, Rachel. You sold the house."

Rachel froze like the birds that had sensed danger. She hadn't talked to Daniel in two or three years. Last time she had, he told her he was marrying an understudy actress from Broadway. Somewhere he had never taken her, but Randall had. Rachel thought of the days she spent with Randall in the city.

"Daniel. What do you want?"

"You sold the house for a pretty penny. Then you up and moved to Texas. I just want my portion from the sale. It's in the divorce papers. If you sell the house, I get half of the money."

"It has been fifteen years, Daniel. We have both moved on. And you only paid alimony for a few months. Why would you think you should get half from the house, especially now? We've already closed on it, for Pete's sake."

"It's in the divorce, Rachel. Check the fine print. I know

you sold the house for way more than we bought it for. I figure I get three or four hundred thousand."

Rachel fumed. "And I paid the mortgage after you left. You get nothing."

"I'm calling my attorney. We'll find your new address. Then I'll file papers. I'll sue you for breach of contract and take everything you have. Might even tap into your rich boyfriend, too. Yeah, I heard all about him. See ya in court, babe." The call disconnected, leaving Rachel shaken.

Rachel made it to the ranch and sat in the car for a few minutes, wiping tears from her face. How had Daniel heard about the house? Probably from the title company, since they had power of attorney to sign for him. Why hadn't they said anything about giving Daniel half the money? She wiped her face again furiously, angry at the turn of events. She thought she had put her ex to rest a long time ago. And she earned what she made from the house. She had made most of the payments. Not Daniel. She finally got out of the car, still shaken.

Randall saw her from the porch and immediately made his way to her, trotting down the steps and wrapping those strong arms around her, pulling her head to his chest. She sobbed into his shirt, shaking as she did. Her feet moved on their own as he guided her up the steps and through the front door to the living area, where they sat on the couch with his arms still around her. She heard him speak softly to Matthew. Then she heard Matthew call Annie, asking her to come over quickly.

"Matthew. Ask her to bring the divorce papers. She knows where they are. And the closing papers on the house, too."

"What's going on, Rachel?" Matthew handed her a box of tissues and a glass of water.

"I'll tell you when Annie gets here. I need a minute to think, first."

"Is everything okay?"

Rachel shook her head, fresh sobs pouring out from her. Randall tucked her in close to his chest again. She appreciated the smell of sunshine, horse, and leather, mingled with whatever made Randall's scent unique. But what would he say when he heard what Daniel was doing?

Car tires crunched on gravel. In another minute, the front door opened and closed, voices talking softly. Annie and Matthew. Something was up with those two. But at this point, she didn't care. Her own life was falling apart. Maybe Annie's too, once she heard the news.

Annie walked into the room and rushed to sit next to her on the couch, placing a packet on the coffee table in front of them. Her daughter hugged her from the other side, squeezing tight. It gave Rachel a boost of confidence.

"Mom? What's going on? Why do you need the papers?"

Rachel sat up and dried her eyes. Pushing her hair back off her forehead, she knew she looked like a mess. She took a deep breath and faced Annie, telling her about the phone call.

Randall stood, his fists at his side. Rachel thought for a minute he was angry at her. This would be the end of their relationship.

"That cheating louse can't do this." He paced the room. "I'll call my attorney. We'll make him pay."

"He said he would sue you too, Randall. I don't know what he hopes to get, or why he thinks he should get anything from you." Rachel took a sip of water that Matthew had set on the coffee table.

"Mom, let's look through the papers together." Annie picked up the packet, pulling out the documents. "There is a lot here, and I know he didn't pay his alimony like he was supposed to, but you didn't press him about it back then, either. You said you wanted to be completely independent from him."

"Let me see the paper. Please."

Rachel watched as Annie handed Matthew the packet and he scanned the pages, flipping through the stack. "There is a section for Disposition of Property. It does say that if the house is sold, the proceeds are split between you." Matthew grimaced.

"Let me see that, Matthew." Randall took the document, read it, and shook his head. "This must be wrong. There has to be a statute of limitations or something. We'll have to check on what the New York laws are, since that is where the divorce was executed."

"I just searched the internet for information. This article from an attorney says that New York is an equitable distribution state. The judge decides what is fair. And there are a lot of factors that are considered. I think you've got a good case, Mom. But you will have to fight it." Annie turned her phone to show Rachel the website.

"Save that info, Annie. I'll call my attorney and see if we can meet with him tomorrow morning." Rachel raised an eyebrow at Randall. "Let me rephrase that. I would like to help, if that is okay with you." Her eyes blurred as Randall laid his forehead on hers.

Rachel twisted her face in an ironic smile. "I would like that. Please. I don't know what else to do, anyway."

"Yes, dear. I'll call my attorney. Is it okay if I make a copy of the document?"

She rolled her eyes at his concession. "Sure." Even though the situation was tense, he was learning his lesson. And she felt better now that she knew she had Randall and his legal team on her side.

Two days passed before they were able to meet with Randall's attorney. Randall had done his best to try to console Rachel, but she knew he was just as livid as she was. They spent Saturday and Sunday watching movies together while Matthew and Annie looked through Rachel's files for anything else pertaining to her property or the divorce. They came up empty.

· ———— ·

RACHEL SHOOK Marcus's hand after Randall guided her into the conference room where they would all meet to discuss Daniel's claim. Randall kept his hand low on her back. Annie asked to attend in support of her mother, and Matthew joined them as well. They told Rachel they were all in this together for her.

After explaining the issue to Marcus, they sat quietly while he reviewed the divorce decree. He raised his head, looking at Rachel.

"Do you have any other documents? Such as a quit claim deed?"

"What's that?" Rachel squinted her eyes in thought.

"That is a document that says Daniel gives up any rights to the property. At any time in the past fifteen years, has he ever signed anything like that?"

"Nothing since the divorce. And I signed so many documents at the closing, I'm honestly not sure what was in there."

Randall took Rachel's hand and squeezed. "So what do we do now, Marcus?"

"Let me request copies of the divorce proceedings that were filed in New York, as well as the sale of the house from the title company."

"The family from Japan moved in right after closing. What will this do to them?"

"This shouldn't affect them. This is about how the proceeds of the sale were distributed. If Daniel didn't get anything from the sale, and we don't have the proper paperwork to prove he no longer had any rights to the proceeds, then we will go to court and a judge will decide."

Randall nodded. "I feel responsible for this, since I suggested the house to the General Manager for VacaRentals. I'll loop him in to make sure nothing slipped through the cracks there." He squeezed Rachel's hand again. "You know, we could just pay him off. It might be just as easy to settle. Less stressful for you." He directed a meaningful gaze at her.

"No. I am tired of being run over. Can we afford to fight him?" Her look was at Marcus. How much would this cost? Would it be worth it?

Randall answered. "We will do whatever you want, sweetheart. Texas men take care of their women."

"I'm here too, Mom." Annie placed a hand on Rachel's arm.

"I am as well, Mrs. Wilson." Matthew spoke softly but surely. Rachel saw the affectionate look pass between Annie and Matthew.

She cried as they all gathered in a group hug. Then Randall's statement sunk in. "Their women." Randall had just called Rachel his woman.

•———•

A WEEK LATER, Marcus called and asked for another meeting. There was no quit claim on file. How had that happened? How had the finance company earlier, and then the title company later, both overlooked such a crucial element? It was turning into a big mess, and Rachel wasn't sure she had the strength to fight. Maybe she should just give Daniel the money he wanted, and maybe he would go away. She had invested most of the proceeds and would have to contact her new financial advisor, but maybe it was the best solution all around. A court case would get ugly and stretch out for months. Or years.

She was too tense to ride Royal. He detected every nerve in her body, which showed in how he handled. Astro was her saving grace. She responded to Rachel as if she completely understood, and they flew across the fields together, Rachel finding sweet release as she rode. Sometimes Randall rode with her. Other times a ranch hand followed a safe distance behind. She didn't really need an escort, but Randall wouldn't have it any other way. He told her he wanted to make sure she stayed safe, and she decided not to fight him on it.

They finally got a court date in New York two months away. That would put them into winter. Randall made travel arrangements for the four of them. Marcus had his admin make arrangements for himself and his paralegal. They would go up a couple of days in advance to meet with Daniel's attorneys. A settlement would be the best route, but the thought of letting him win caused bile to rise in Rachel's throat. She didn't understand why Daniel was doing this, but she knew she couldn't trust him when they divorced, and she didn't trust him now.

Randall had been rock solid for her. He always asked before making any arrangements, suggesting rather than telling her what she needed to do. She grew more in love with him every day, but neither one of them had said the full three-word phrase yet. Randall had hinted, though.

He met her at the stable, taking Astro's reins before she dismounted. "You rode her hard today." Astro had sweat rings around her neck and saddle.

"Thank you for riding with me, Tyler." Rachel stopped the cowboy before he left. "I'm sorry I tried to leave you in the dust." Tyler was a ranch hand that had already ridden with her several times. She knew that he or any of the other cowboys could probably ride rings around her, and he politely let her lead as they rode along.

"No problem, Miss Rachel." Tyler grinned. "It was fun trying to keep up with you. I'm glad you enjoyed your ride. Let me take Astro and I'll rub her down for you." He tipped his beat-up black hat and walked away, guiding both horses to the back of the barn.

Rachel turned to Randall. "He's a schmoozer. Kept me in stitches when I wasn't trying to run away."

"Yeah, he has his ways." Rachel wondered what Randall meant by that. She watched the cowboy swagger away, guessing that was a story for another day.

• •—————• •

"I GOT a call from Marcus today. The title company says there was no quit claim on file, but the calculations showed Daniel wasn't due anything. I'm not sure what that means. But I told them to do whatever was necessary. Is that okay?"

"You know, Randall, normally I would be upset at you for stepping in without asking, but I am learning that sometimes it is better to be grateful. So thank you. This has been stressful enough. You have taken a lot of the burden on your shoulders, and I just want to say how much I appreciate that." She laid her hand on his chest, playing with a button on the pocket over his heart.

Randall stepped closer, hoping her actions were an invitation, and wrapped one arm around her waist. Tipping her head up with his finger, he studied her face. Her blue eyes were wide, the soft wrinkles there evidence of time and experience. He smoothed his thumb over one of them before leaning in to kiss it, loving each one. When she closed her eyes, he kissed the other side. Then he took her face in both hands and softly touched her lips with his.

"I hope you know I love you, Rachel."

She responded with a kiss of her own that showed him her heart with the depth of the kiss. He knew she wasn't quite ready to put her feelings into words, but her kiss confirmed everything. They danced around each other, kissing, looking into each other's eyes, kissing again, and turning in circles as he took her in his arms and moved her around the floor between the stalls in a slow, silent, two-step.

• •————————• •

MARCUS CAME to the ranch the following week to review the case with them again. Annie and Matthew were also meeting with them, so they met in Randall's office where there was a small conference table in addition to the desk. He looked around the room at the four of them, focusing his attention back on Rachel.

"According to the closing statement, this was all calculated during the closing. There was no quit claim, but there was also nothing due to Daniel. The divorce decree says the distribution would be the total house sale, minus any realtor, title, or recording fees, minus the payoff on the remaining mortgage, minus any unpaid alimony. Anything left would be split fifty-fifty."

"Daniel is claiming that I chose to forego alimony in order to keep the house. He paid alimony for about six months, then stopped. I didn't press it because I had gotten my job and quite honestly, I didn't want anything else to do with him. But I paid the mortgage every month after the divorce, not Daniel."

Rachel recalled Daniel's phone call, furious that this was happening.

"And you didn't refinance after the divorce?"

"No. I guess that was an oversight on my part."

"Your attorney should have recommended that. So the oversight is on his side. But now Daniel is saying that the deduction for unpaid alimony should not have been taken, and he is due his share. Did you have anything in writing saying he could stop the alimony?"

"No. I guess we should have done that, too." She looked up at Randall, frustrated at the items that were overlooked during both the divorce and the sale of the house.

"How much did he owe?"

"Fifteen years' worth because I never remarried. Over two hundred thousand dollars." She looked at Annie, and her daughter grabbed her hand and squeezed.

"And that's what he's now claiming you owe him?"

Rachel nodded. "That, or more. Maybe three or four, he said. I don't know where he is getting his numbers."

"How long did he make the payments on the house?"

"Ten years. We had a thirty-year mortgage. There was five years left when the house was sold."

Matthew jumped into the conversation. "Payments at the front of the mortgage are usually all interest and very little principal. Rachel would have paid much more on the principal portion of the loan than Daniel would have paid."

"How did the house sell without the quit claim?" Randall held his index finger in the air as he asked the question, head tilted in thought.

"Turns out he gave the title company power of attorney to sign for him. I guess he thought he would still get a share." Marcus shook his head.

Rachel turned to Randall, anger in her eyes. "This is all a

big mess! I should never have sold the house. I should have stayed in New York. I can't—do this again." She gripped her hair, palms over her ears, then let go. "I just want to go back to my home. Back to my job. Back to my *life*. And now all of that is gone." She stormed out of the office. Annie followed, while Randall watched her go.

As she was leaving, she heard Randall plead to his attorney, "You have to fix this, man. She means the world to me. I can't lose her."

Maybe they had both already lost.

TWENTY-FOUR

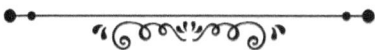

SIX WEEKS PASSED. Rachel stayed away from the ranch, unsure of herself and the direction her life had taken. Randall visited her at the condo, and they spent those days sitting together on the davenport. But Rachel refused to discuss the case or their future.

It was a Friday evening, and they were sitting on the balcony watching the traffic, as cars drove down the small street in front of the condo. Some had loud music playing, the bass pounding a beat that could be heard a block away. It mirrored the turmoil in Rachel's soul.

Randall placed his arm around Rachel's shoulder and pulled her closer to him. She laid her head on him, drawing strength from his support. He had been a rock so far, and had reviewed every point and decision with her—as much as she would allow. She really didn't want to talk about it, even though she knew they had to.

"We fly to New York next week. Are you ready for this?"

Rachel snuggled into the blanket he had brought out to her. "I just wish it was over."

"Marcus said we should make a final offer. If he doesn't accept a settlement, we go before a judge."

"He doesn't deserve a dime."

"I know that, and you know that. A judge may see differently. It would be better if we can settle before it gets to that point."

"Why are you doing this, Randall? What is your motive? This isn't your battle. And I know Marcus can't come cheap. His time costs money, too." Rachel lifted her chin, still leaning against his shoulder.

"The battle is mine because I love you, Rachel. I wouldn't have it any other way. If you had sold your house to that other couple, you still might have this problem. Daniel is a louse, and you deserve a man who will treat you with respect. I want to be that man for you, the one you should have had all along." He stroked her hair with his fingers, twisting a curl as he did.

"I have trust issues, Randall." It was a simple statement that made him chuckle.

"Oh, I'm well aware of that, darlin.' I love you anyway." He kissed her temple, then turned her face to his and kissed her again.

•————••

MONDAY MORNING, Rachel, Randall, and Annie boarded their direct flight for New York, settling into their first-class seats. Marcus and his paralegal had flown up the night before, and Matthew stayed home to take care of ranch operations. Randall wanted to charter a private jet for all of them, but Rachel nixed that idea, saying the whole fiasco was costing enough, as it was.

Randall squeezed Rachel's hand, looking around her to Annie to get her attention, speaking to both of them. "When we get there, I have a limo waiting for us, and we'll take the scenic route to the city so we can check into the hotel. I booked a block of suites for all of us. Then I will take the two most beautiful ladies on the earth to a nice steak dinner at the restaurant where I signed our new contract. Jolly will want to meet you."

"Jolly? That's a strange name. I don't think you ever told me that."

"Yeah, his parents were rather free spirits. They named him Jolly because he had such a happy face when he was born."

"So that is his real name?" Annie leaned over to speak.

"That is his real name. And he really is a happy guy. I don't think I've ever heard him complain about anything in the entire time I've known him."

The flight landed on time, and the limo was luxurious, stocked with Rachel's favorite sweet tea and chocolates. Randall pointed out attractions they had seen when he had made the first trip, but she was glad for the distraction, keeping her mind off the next day's meeting.

The hotel was a nineteenth-century landmark overlooking the south side of Central Park. Rachel marveled at the elaborate décor in the lobby. Marble floors throughout, decorated with plush wool rugs that looked hand-stitched. Chandeliers that would rival any found in Buckingham Palace. Off-white paneled walls and a ceiling at least sixteen feet high, were painted in delicate gold filigree.

The registration clerk handed a bellhop the room keys, who guided them to a private elevator off the main lobby, telling them their bags would be brought up just a few minutes behind them by another bellhop. The elevator was richly decorated with dark walnut paneling, and Rachel started adding up numbers in her head.

They stepped out of the elevator into a small alcove, where two large double doors stood open in welcome. Rachel gasped and heard Annie do the same.

"Is this the penthouse? Randall, please tell me you didn't." She turned to him and placed her hand on his arm, eyes wide.

"Yes, I did." His eyes twinkled. "You deserve the best. And there are two bedrooms. One with a king, the other with two queen beds. So there is plenty of room for the three of us."

She watched as Randall slipped a bill into the bellhop's hand and the young man's face lit up in pleasure. It must have been no small tip.

"Oh, Mom! Come look at the view! This is incredible!" Annie giggled as she waved Rachel over to the large bank of windows in the sitting area between the rooms.

Rachel took in the view of the park below and stood frozen, her hand to her mouth, as Randall came up behind her. She turned back to him suddenly, wrapping her arms around his waist, and swiped a tear that had leaked from one eye. She had no words to say. She was simply overwhelmed.

•⸱————————•⸱•

RANDALL HELD his hand to Rachel's back as they entered the restaurant, which was connected to the hotel by a small hallway. At the desk, he handed the hostess a business card, and she smiled at them.

"Right this way, Mr. Hudson. Jolly will be out soon." She led them to a table in a small alcove with a window looking out into Times Square, and Randall held Rachel's chair out for her as they sat.

"Randall! It is so good to see you again, my friend! And you are escorting two beautiful young ladies!"

"Jolly, I would like you to meet the love of my life, Rachel Wilson, and Annie, her daughter. Ladies, this is Jolly."

"Finally! I am happy to meet you both!" Grinning at Rachel he said, "You have put a twinkle in this man's eyes that has been gone too long."

"It is nice to meet you, Jolly. You have a beautiful restaurant."

"And it is lovely ladies like you and your daughter that make it so. Welcome to my humble eatery."

There was nothing humble about it. A large main dining room was surrounded by smaller, private booths, the décor similar to the hotel lobby. Upstairs were meeting rooms and more private areas, such as the one they were sitting in now. The lighting was low and intimate, even though the chandeliers reflected the light throughout the room.

"This meal is on the house tonight. Please feel free to enjoy anything from the menu. It is my pleasure, as it makes me joyful to see my old friend so happy."

Rachel turned to Randall after Jolly left, placing her hand over his. "How long have you known Jolly? I was under the impression this was a new business venture for the ranch."

"Jolly and I met at a Cattlemen's convention when we were both in our twenties. His family had a small ranch farther south than ours, closer to the border. When his parents died, he sold the ranch and moved to New York to become a chef. He just bought the restaurant last year and contacted me as soon as he did. We had to wait for the existing beef contract to expire before we could sign a new one. I think I'm going to like being his business partner."

"But you just supply the beef, right?"

"Well, I have an interest in the restaurant, too. But I'm a silent partner, except for the beef. The restaurant is all Jolly's."

Rachel wondered how many business ventures Randall was involved in. Maybe she wouldn't worry so much about the cost of this trip.

TWENTY-FIVE

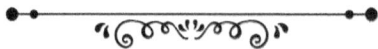

RANDALL AND MARCUS insisted on meeting at a neutral location, preferring that over the hostile location of Daniel's attorney's office. Rachel was glad they were not meeting at the hotel. She was afraid that if Daniel saw where she was staying, in all that opulence, he would press for even more than his original request. He didn't deserve anything. She had paid the mortgage, or at least most of it. They calculated that Daniel had paid less than fifteen percent of the principal, and that was while they were married. Rachel had scrimped and saved to make sure they didn't lose the house after the divorce. She wasn't going to sell and give him half. What bothered her the most was, why was he doing this now?"

The only thing she could determine was that Daniel had learned who owned VacaRentals, and that Randall had orchestrated the sale and subsequent purchase. And that Randall was worth more money than Rachel would ever hope to see in her lifetime. Daniel was a predator, pure and simple. But Rachel was not like the birds that had frozen. He would find that out soon.

They walked into the rented conference room in a downtown office building. The walls were granite, the décor cold. Good. This would be a much better environment. They checked in with the receptionist at the front desk, who then called for a security guard to escort them to their room.

Randall had ordered catering for their morning meeting. The pastries smelled freshly baked and made Rachel's stomach grumble. Coffee was available in insulated carafes, along with orange juice and water. But even though her stomach said she was hungry, she was really just nervous. Marcus arrived while she was looking out a window at the city around them, and began setting up his laptop, logging into the room's video system.

Daniel and his attorney arrived just before their appointed time. He had a smug look on his face as everyone shook hands around the table. Rachel tried to ignore him and noticed Annie doing the same. She hated that Annie was in the middle, but was glad that her daughter was standing with her.

Daniel smirked at Rachel. "I hope there are no hard feelings, babe. I had to strike while the iron was hot."

"Yeah, well, I brought a fire extinguisher." Rachel glared at her ex. Randall took her hand in his to calm her. But the action made Daniel grin wider. It was an evil grin she had seen on his face during their divorce. She would not cave to him.

Marcus took control. "Why don't we all have a seat?" Daniel's attorney whispered something into Daniel's ear, and the pair sat down on the opposite side of the table.

"Mr. Wilson," Marcus spoke again. "We have prepared an accounting of all payments regarding the mortgage for the property in question, as well as the alimony paid and owed." He displayed the calculations on the large monitor that hung from the wall.

"As you can see by our sums here, you paid a very small amount on the mortgage, proportionally speaking, compared to what Mrs. Wilson has paid in succeeding years. When the alimony is factored in, the resulting balance is less than zero. However, we have decided to make a good faith offer, and are prepared to offer a settlement in the sum of fifty thousand dollars. In return, you will sign a document foregoing any additional funds from Mrs. Wilson, or her daughter Annie, for any reason whatsoever. This includes any further complaints or suits, regardless of change in future status.

You will also agree to forego any suits against Hudson Holdings for any reason associated with Mrs. Wilson, Annie, or any business conducted in the state of New York."

Marcus stared at Daniel. "We believe this offer is exceptional, and you should—as they say—take the money and run."

"Annie is my daughter too. You can't keep me away from her. Money or otherwise." Daniel sputtered, his jaw stiff.

"Father. You have not—not once—reached out to me since the divorce. I will not be your pawn." Rachel smiled at Annie's response. Her girl had fire in her.

"Will you excuse us a moment, please?" Daniel's attorney placed his hand on Daniel's shoulder as a signal to stop speaking.

"Certainly. There is a connected room where you can speak privately." Marcus pointed to a separate door on one side of the room.

Rachel blew out a breath as the pair went into the other room, closing the door behind them. "What now? Do you think they will take the offer?"

"They would be fools not to," Randall spoke up. "Our numbers are solid. I don't see how a judge would ever rule in his favor, especially since he gave the title company power of attorney to act on his behalf at the closing. This may seem excessive on our part, but it will guarantee that this lunacy will end, and that Daniel will never bother you again. For any reason." He patted Rachel's hand before taking her fingers in his. "Would you like some coffee or juice?"

"Maybe some juice, please." She tapped the fingers on her other hand in rapid succession on the table before Annie gently stopped her.

"I'll get it for Mom." She looked over Rachel at Randall, her eyes saying, 'Stay here and keep her calm.'

Daniel and his attorney returned several minutes later. Returning to their seats, Daniel's attorney spoke. "Mr. Wilson has a counteroffer. One hundred thousand dollars. One-time settlement. And he will agree to all of your stipulations."

Rachel rose from her seat in horror. Randall placed his hand on hers again, urging her to sit down. His eyes seemed to tell her that everything would be all right.

"We were prepared for this." Marcus was speaking now. "While we think your demands are beyond excessive, we are prepared to agree—if for no other reason than to give Mrs. Wilson closure."

Looking at Randall, Rachel tried to shake her head *No*, but Randall patted her hand. It would be okay. Daniel was the hawk, the predator, but he would be gone, and they could go back to their lives without fear he would return.

She watched in a daze as Randall pulled a certified check from his shirt pocket. It was already made out to Daniel. All parties shook hands, although Rachel avoided shaking hands with her ex. She didn't know Randall had come with a check already prepared. She should be making that payment. She will have to pay him back.

Documents were signed by both sides, and notarized by a representative provided by the office complex. Daniel stuck the check in a leather binder and walked from the room, leaving his attorney behind.

A LIMO WAS WAITING OUTSIDE for them as they left the office building, but Annie walked to a waiting cab.

"Where are you going, Annie? The limo is over here."

"I'm flying home tonight, Mom. Randall made arrangements for me. You guys have fun."

Rachel turned to Randall, her what-are-you-doing-now look in full force on her face. "What are you two up to?"

"Annie asked if she could go home early. I think she is wanting to get home to Matthew a day sooner."

"What about her luggage?"

"I had it delivered from the hotel to the airport."

"There is something going on between them, isn't there?"

"I believe so." Randall wiggled his eyebrows and gestured toward the limo. "The night is ours, grand lady. What would you like to do? Dinner, dancing, another show, or maybe something else?" The drive back to the hotel was short. They could have walked, but Randall didn't want to wear Rachel out in the event she wanted to do something together tonight.

"How about dinner? After that, surprise me." Rachel looked happy. The worry lines were gone, replaced with a smile that dazzled his heart.

"All right. I do have something in mind."

"I thought you probably did."

"Great. Let's get back to the hotel, rest a bit, then we have reservations at six o'clock at a very nice restaurant that I think you will enjoy.

THE NIGHT AIR was cool but not cold as they walked the short distance to the restaurant. It was American cuisine, but the atmosphere was a hodgepodge of décor from around the world, representing the many cultures that made up New York City. They ordered an Asian concoction that neither of them could pronounce, but it melted in their mouths, and they shared it between them.

Sitting side by side in a private booth, Randall wrapped his arm around Rachel, kissing her temple lightly.

"Randall, can you hand my bag to me, please?"

When he did, she opened a front pocket and pulled out a check, handing it to him.

"What's this?" He opened the check, noting the amount.

"You'll have to wait a couple of days before I can move the money. So don't cash it just yet."

"I don't want this, Rachel." He tried to stuff it back into her purse.

"Randall, the settlement is my responsibility. Please don't fight me on this."

"Woman." He closed his eyes and took a breath before reopening them. "Let's not discuss this here. I'll put the check in my pocket—for now." He pulled out his phone and sent a quick message to somebody.

As they left the restaurant, a horse-drawn carriage pulled up. "Mr. Hudson?" The driver addressed them as they walked up.

"Yes. Thanks for your promptness." He helped Rachel climb into the carriage and followed behind her. A cold breeze blew, swirling fallen leaves, so he unfolded the blanket that he found on the seat and tucked it around them, wrapping his arms around Rachel as he did. He nodded, and the driver reined the horses into the traffic.

"We're going to drive around Central Park. I thought you might enjoy seeing it from a different perspective."

Rachel nodded but stayed quiet, leaning her head on his shoulder. He could feel her muscles tense, and he suspected she was deciding how to bring up the subject of the check again. He decided to speak first.

"I wasn't going to do this quite this soon. But you know I love you. I haven't made any secret about that." He heard Rachel draw in a breath and continued quickly.

"I'm not proposing tonight. But I do want to talk about it."

"Okay." He almost missed her quiet response.

"At some point, hopefully in the near future, I hope you will agree to change your name from Wilson to Hudson. What's mine will be yours. So you see, there is no need to pay back the settlement. That is what you are trying to do, right?"

Rachel nodded, still quiet.

He hugged her closer, both arms around her.

"When the time is right—when you are ready—you can propose to me. I promise I will say yes. But I know you have been independent for a very long time, and too many decisions have been taken out of your hands lately. This decision, and the timing, will be yours. I'll wait. As long as it takes."

"You don't want a prenup?"

"Why? I'm all in, Rachel. I trust you."

Randall felt a tear drop from Rachel's cheek onto his chest. He kissed the top of her head and rubbed his hand up and down her arm before nipping an earlobe. "We're gonna have to put some diamonds in those ears. Make 'em sparkle." He chuckled and wrapped his arms around her again, snuggling them both under the blanket.

Rachel stirred in his arms. "Nobody has loved me like this.

Daniel certainly didn't. I don't know what I have done to deserve you, but I love you too, Randall Hudson." She raised her head and kissed him gently on his jawline. He bent his head to meet her lips with his. The rest of the ride was spent as lovers do, enjoying the taste and scent of each other as the park faded into the distance.

TWENTY-SIX

THIS MAN. This infuriatingly wonderful hunk of a cowboy. As at home in business negotiations as he is on his horse, riding alongside her across the ranch. What was she going to do with him? She froze in her thoughts as she glanced at the man sleeping with his head against the window. They were once again in first-class on their return trip home.

Randall had been by her side all along, even when she was mad at him. His intentions were pure, even if his methods were wrong. He was a first-class man all the way—in traveling and in life. She would be a fool to let him slip away from her.

They touched down in San Antonio after staying three more days in New York. They had eaten at Jolly's again, gone to a Broadway show, and visited the Statue of Liberty. He wined and dined her, and she finally relaxed.

Annie and Matthew met them at the airport. Annie was beaming when she hugged them, glowing as she looked over their shoulders at Matthew.

"We have a surprise for you, Mom!" The diamond on

Annie's finger glittered under the airport skylight as Annie wiggled the fingers on her left hand.

"You're getting married!" Rachel and Annie both squealed and hugged again while Randall and Matthew looked sheepishly at each other. Did Randall know about this? Of course! Matthew must have told him about his plans.

They all walked together to the baggage claim area. Not too long ago, Rachel had come to Texas with more baggage than she knew what to do with. Emotional baggage. Randall had claimed it, and her heart. She glanced sideways at the man who now meant more to her than life itself. If she had taken a different trip—Alaska or Jamaica, as she and Annie had briefly discussed—she would have missed out on the most wonderful thing to ever happen to her, aside from her daughter Annie. He was strong, stoic, and hers.

Back at the condo, Annie pounced on Rachel. "So? How did it go? I expected you to come home with a ring on your finger, too." Annie wiggled her eyebrows.

They sat together on the couch, talking about their respective dates. Somehow, they had been blessed enough to find two good men. Rachel told Annie about the carriage ride.

"He told you he wasn't going to propose to you, but that he would say yes if you proposed to him? That is the craziest idea ever—and I love it! He really gets you, Mom."

"Well, it was a little rocky there for a while." Rachel pushed back a blue curl of hair.

"Yes, but he learned his lesson and applied it very wisely. What are you going to do?"

"I don't know. If you're marrying Matthew, that will leave me alone here at the condo. I'm not sure I want that now."

"That's not a good reason for getting married, Mom. You taught me that."

Rachel sighed, laying her head back on the couch. Turning

her head to look at her daughter, she smiled. "I love him, Annie. And I know he loves me, too."

"Then what's holding you back?"

"Well, this thing with Daniel was holding me back."

"And now it's resolved." Annie gave her mother a parental look.

"You're right. The only thing holding me back, I guess, is me."

THREE WEEKS PASSED by in a blur. Randall and Matthew stayed busy with several business ventures, including the purchase of a new Dutch Warmblood mare to mate with Royal. Her name was Regal Princess, and Rachel had immediately fallen in love with her.

Annie was working on a marketing project for a new client. She was also working on wedding plans, keeping the ceremony short and simple. They would marry in two months.

Rachel took on an impromptu role of hostess for the guests that visited each week. She loved the interaction with them, and the stories that brought them to the ranch. But something was still missing, and she knew what that something was.

This morning, the winter weather had stepped aside, allowing a hint of warmth to blanket the ranch. The sun had just risen over the stables as she strode out to ride Astro. It was her favorite thing to do on the ranch, and she didn't mind making the drive each day from the condo. The time at sunrise was peaceful as the ranch woke up and the various activities began. Cows mooed, an old rooster crowed, and horses munched grass as the pre-dawn turned to a brighter shade of pink. It was a far cry from New York. She had finally found her home.

"Good morning, beautiful lady. Are you ready for your ride?" She had asked Randall to join her today. His grin stretched across his face.

"God is good. The ranch is beautiful, and I'm with the most wonderful man in the world. Yes, I'm ready." Rachel smiled, suddenly shy.

They rode to their favorite picnic spot under the cotton-woods that grew by the smaller lake. It was a couple of miles back on the ranch. Beautiful, quiet, and private.

They spread out a red and black plaid blanket on the bank of the lake, and he pulled her into his lap, his arms wrapped around her. She inhaled deeply, breathing in the scent of the beauty around her, and the man with her. His perfect scent.

A woodpecker pecked out a staccato beat, searching for bugs. Robins tweeted, and bluejays squawked. A squirrel ran down the side of another tree, looked at them, then turned and scampered away. A soft breeze blew this morning, flipping her hair into her face. She pushed it back, and it fell again. She finally gave up.

"Randall, I have a problem, and I don't know what to do about it." She put an exasperated look on her face.

He turned her sideways to face him. "Your hair is beautiful. Stop fussing with it."

"That's not the problem." But she pushed her hair back again. She was nervous.

"What is the problem then, darlin'? It's not that louse again, is it? He was supposed to go away."

"Oh, no, it's not him." She quickly steered away from that topic. This was supposed to be a romantic moment.

Randall took her face in his calloused hands, staring into

her eyes, his gaze sliding back and forth between them. "What is it?"

His warm brown eyes gave her courage. This is where she belonged. She cupped his exquisite jawline with one hand, caressing a wrinkle with her thumb. She looked down. Then looked back up. Took another breath. He continued to study her face while he waited.

"Well," she swallowed. "There's this man, see. And I've kind of fallen in love with him. And I really want to ask him to marry me, but I don't know how." She returned his gaze, hoping he understood what she was saying.

"It's simple, Rachel. Just ask him." His voice was rough with emotion.

Rachel twisted from his lap onto both knees, and took both of his hands in hers. The sun broke over the horizon as all her worries broke free in her mind. "Randall, I love you with all my heart, and I can't imagine what the future would look like without you in it. Will you marry me? Please?"

She watched as his face glowed in a way she had never seen before. He took his hat off, setting it on the ground, and pulled a ring from a shirt pocket. The one over his heart. "I hoped this was why you asked me to ride with you this morning."

"So that's a yes?" Rachel was stunned at the size of the ring that he slipped onto her finger. The clear, flawless diamond was square, with smaller diamonds on each side.

"Yes, darlin'," His voice was filled with emotion. "A million times, yes. And it's about time. I feel like I've been waiting *forever*."

She laughed as he pulled her off her knees, rolling her onto her back to kiss her senseless. They stayed there all morning, loving each other and making plans. Rachel had told Annie what she was doing, so nobody would miss them today. Maybe they could have a double wedding. Father and son marrying mother and daughter. What a way to make a family.

EPILOGUE

THE RANCH BUZZED with excitement as most of the town gathered at the gazebo by the main lake. Tables full of refreshments were set up along one side of the chairs, which were already full. Even though it was early spring and the breeze was nippy, there was standing room only.

Neither Randall nor Matthew had requested a prenup. They both said that was preparation for ending a marriage that hadn't even started. They wanted their brides to know their vows would be forever. Father and son stood together next to the preacher, serving as the best man for each other. They were dressed similar to the way Randall had dressed in New York. Black jeans, starched white button-down shirts, gray suit jackets with western stitching on the shoulders and sleeves, and mother-of-pearl bolo ties. Black hats and boots completed the look.

A soft guitar played a ballad meant for lovers as Rachel and Annie walked down the aisle together. Their dresses were simple and elegant. Soft, off-white silk, draping over their curves to a length just above the ground. Small lacy hats tilted to one side of their heads. They wore flat leather slippers, also off-white, and held bouquets of wildflowers in their hands.

Cheers rose up from the guests as the preacher announced them each man and wife. Husbands kissed their wives, an exaggerated dip making the crowd whoop before they strolled down the aisle. The reception would be held at the barn, where there would be an evening of food and dancing for everyone.

TYLER STOOD to one side of the barn, watching as everyone celebrated. He had escorted Rachel on several rides and thought Randall made a good choice. Randall was the only one who knew Tyler's story. Even Matthew didn't know all of it. He watched as a cute little pixie with brilliant green eyes congratulated the couples. Something had been stirring in his soul for a while, and he continued to watch as she made her way around the room, greeting several people.

"She's out of bounds, man." His best friend and fellow cowboy, Reggie, nudged him with his elbow. "Come on. Let's find some party girls to dance with."

They twirled the floor with several pretty girls—as many as possible. But Tyler noticed when the green-eyed pixie left the reception. He knew who she was. Everyone knew her. He blew out a breath and turned back to the party, ready for more boot-scootin.' But something settled in his heart, and he knew they would meet. Soon.

THE END

AUTHOR'S NOTE

Thank you for reading A Matter of Trust. There are a lot of clean romance books for twenty and thirty-somethings, but few for middle-aged adults. Randall and Rachel both found a place in my heart as I told their story. Or more accurately, they told their story to me. I'm just the scribe.

Nora Hills, Texas is a fictional town based on a small town southwest of Fort Worth. Glen Rose is a sleepy place, full of bright characters. Rodeo is also a favorite pastime there. If you ever travel through the area, make sure to stop by Debbie's Restaurant and say "Hi" to the guys at the real Table of Knowledge. My characters here are a bit of a compilation, not based on any one person. But the real-life men are just as fun.

Stay tuned for my next book in this series. I'm sure you will grow to love Tyler as he searches for purpose, and finds love in the process.

ALSO BY RENA BELL YEAGER

Nora Hills Texas Series

A Matter of Trust – Rachel and Randall, a Nora Hills prequel

Rumors of Grace – Tyler and Georgia

Promise of Honor – Reggie and Haley

A Place of Peace – Ritz and Peyton

Whispers of Hope – Malcolm and Emily

A Thread of Truth – Caleb and Veeve

Standalone

House of Cards

Other Credits

Happy Days, ABC Network, 1974-1984

The Music Man, Broadway Play, Meredith Willson and Franklin Lacey, 1957